Robert Seldon attends the funeral of Edward Stone, another rare book dealer. In Seldon's pocket, as he stands at Stone's graveside, there is a cable from an eccentric American collector offering £500 for the notorious 'Ibiza' Letters which Seldon knows were once in Stone's possession. This sets him off on a picaresque quest which leads to a curious second-hand shop off the Old Kent Road, the dog-ridden home of a Spiritualist, a paper tycoon's mansion in Dorset and a recluse's decaying Thames-side villa.

He has opened 'the terrible door into the past' out of curiosity and a desire to make money, but finds himself being involved more and more deeply in the mystery that surrounds the Letters and which makes him believe that two murders have been committed.

Parallel with his inquiry as to the fate of the Letters there is another journey back into Shakespeare's 'dark backward and abysm of time', shown in a series of flashbacks to the Riviera, Ibiza and war-time London and Naples, for Seldon is also dominated by events in the past. As he goes to a strange appointment on Westminster Bridge, to make love to a sex-starved widow, to pursue a dead man, to an idyllic meeting with the tycoon's beautiful daughter, to a Bohemian party and a hectic chase and fight in the London streets, Seldon is freeing himself of depression and despair by becoming absorbed in other people's problems.

*George Sims (1923–1999) served in the Army Intelligence Corps during WWII and then became a dealer in rare books and manuscripts, a world he exploits to the full in several of his thrillers including his first, **The Terrible Door**. Elected a member of the famous Detection Club, Sims was widely regarded as a master creator of creepy atmospheres in seemingly ordinary settings and his writing has been described as: "distinguished", "high above crime fiction average" and "sinister and unusual".*

Top Notch Thrillers

Ostara Publishing's new imprint **Top Notch Thrillers** aims to revive Great British thrillers, which do not deserve to be forgotten. Each title has been carefully selected not just for its plot or sense of adventure but for the distinctiveness and sheer quality of its writing.

Other Top Notch Thrillers from Ostara Publishing

Philip Purser **Night of Glass**
Geoffrey Rose **Clear Road to Archangel**
Alan Williams **Snake Water**

Top Notch Thrillers

THE
TERRIBLE
DOOR

GEORGE SIMS

Ostara Publishing

All the characters of this story are wholly imaginary and have no reference whatever to actual people

© George Sims 1964

A CIP reference is available from the British Library

Printed and Bound in the United Kingdom

ISBN 9781906288280

Ostara Publishing
13 King Coel Road
Colchester
CO3 9AG
www.ostarapublishing.co.uk

The Series Editor for Top Notch Thrillers is Mike Ripley, author of the award-winning 'Angel' comic thrillers, co-editor of the three *Fresh Blood* anthologies promoting new British crime writing and, for ten years, the crime fiction critic of the *Daily Telegraph*. He currently writes the 'Getting Away With Murder' column for the e-zine *Shots* on www.shotsmag.co.uk.

FOR
BERYL

'The terrible door into the past ...'
Scott Fitzgerald

'We live in fear, and therefore we do not live'
Buddha

1

Across the coffin Goldman's eyes sought mine urgently. When he was sure he had my attention he closed one dark-brown, bloodshot eye and moved his head slowly from side to side. The wink was so serious and meaningful to him yet so meaningless to me that I had to look quickly away, above his head and the others facing me. A little way behind him Tassiter and his small daughter stared at the grave. The little girl was learning fast: only three months before I had read of her mother's death. It was hard to believe that bright, energetic woman was not still at their small house in Crouch End and would never again answer a phone call in her gay, youthful voice. Why had Tassiter come to this dismal affair so soon after his own wife's funeral, and dragged this sad-eyed child along with him? The ceremony obviously had a significance for him that I could not discover.

The January sky at four o'clock was rapidly becoming dark, wind moved restlessly in the line of short leafless trees along the cemetery wall and small bunches of faded flowers were beaten relentlessly down by the rain. As far as I could see rows of uniformly tiled roofs fell away into the gloom of the grey sky. The rain which had been coming in slow drops down my neck had mastered the situation and now ran smoothly in. I jerked my head and tried to concentrate on Stone's grave. Then I put my hand under my raincoat to my jacket pocket and touched the crinkly paper of the cable form. I was looking for a handkerchief but it was not there. I found one in a trouser pocket and wiped some of the rain from my face. As I moved my foot there was a dull chink, and I looked down to see that I'd kicked a grimy jam-jar half-full with water and dead flowers. The slight bump I'd been standing on was a small, neglected grave. There was nothing to mark it except the jar and a tiny hillock of uncut grass.

The wind and the rain and the dark winter sky gave me an overwhelming feeling of futility. I felt that the huddled group of people might as well all fall into the dark hole before us. I moved forward a few inches off the little grave. It was hard to reconcile this gloomy urban plot as being a part of Sandbourne which would be passed by children on their way to the sea in the summer. Not far behind those roofs the sea was keeping to its rhythm of tides. I smiled at Jane Tassiter. My smile was useless to her, but I hated to see her looking so old and wise. It seemed impossible that summer would come again and in a few months children like Jane would be straggling along the road behind us, carefree and happy.

'Remember' – the one echoing word was isolated in my mind from the hurried drone of the tired-looking priest. I regarded Edward Stone's expensive coffin once more and tried to remember a little. I was not as tough as I pretended and the cable in my pocket was not the only reason for overcoming my antipathy to funerals. It was curious that, standing next to Stone's widow and his sister-in-law, I was apparently regarded as a relative or a very close friend by the other mourners, and yet I had only met him for the first time a year before.

It had been at the same time of year, just after Christmas, at a country auction sale in the New Forest. The books I had hoped to buy at the sale had been grossly over-described in the catalogue, but I had stayed on till the end to bid for an attractive collection of drawings of eighteenth-century coaches and carriages. They were brilliantly coloured, and in my enthusiasm I had taken the bidding to seventy-five pounds when a fat, quiet man leaning against a wall had doubled my bid. As soon as the sale was over he came up and introduced himself. I knew him by reputation as being a successful dealer who supplied, a handful of very wealthy collectors. I also knew that he was supposed to be a shy, reserved man.

I had been surprised, therefore, to have an invitation from him at our first meeting to visit his house which he also used as business premises. The house was a commonplace one in a seedy Victorian part of Sandbourne, but it was extremely well furnished and comfortable. Much more money had been spent on it than one would have expected from its exterior and the neighbourhood. His office gleamed with leather arm-chairs and fine oak cases full of rich morocco and calf bindings.

I was surprised too when he introduced me to his wife Margaret: she appeared to be at least fifteen years younger than he. She was plump yet quite strikingly attractive, with a mass of dark red hair; very white, clear skin and large, green eyes. Stone was a plain man with a short, thick neck. His hair was white with a dull yellowish tinge to it, carefully brushed forward and across his wide, deeply lined forehead. His pale face was usually expressionless. He was always fiddling with a pipe, relighting it innumerable times, stuffing tobacco in with stubby, clumsy fingers. He spoke slowly, the sentences often punctuated by the suck and puff of pipe-smoking. I knew that strangers got the impression of a dull, rather boring Yorkshireman. Actually he was shrewd and sensitive.

As I got to know him better I realized that he was pleased by this disguise; indeed I found that he cultivated it. He was a man who liked secrets; it pleased him to attend a country sale and be regarded as slight opposition by local collectors, knowing that he had the knowledge and money to buy every item he wanted.

This was just one of many ways in which we were opposites. My qualities were on the surface: I managed to hide my natural shyness and often dissembled a basic sense of negation with a feigned enthusiasm or gaiety. Some women found me attractive. People who did not know much about books thought I was knowledgeable, but I had no real deep scholarly interest in literature as Stone had. He was calm, serious and methodical: I could not take anything very seriously, and quickly lost interest in things. Our tastes were often opposed: he liked only classical music while I would as soon listen to jazz or swing. But we did share an interest in the books written by Frederick Lupin.

The rain in the cemetery was coming with renewed force on the raw clods of earth, spilling down the sides of the grave, making

9

the clay smooth and shiny. 'Man that is born of woman hath but a short time to live.' Someone by my side was crying. It was Margaret's sister, Ann. The big tears came slowly at first, then her face crumpled in a rictus of fear and sorrow. It was a good time to cry but Margaret's face was drained of expression, her eyes dry and staring at the pit by our feet.

I felt like an emotional bankrupt: an emptiness which was displeasing, because Stone had been a good friend to me. But I found it difficult to connect the heavy body in the wooden box with the person I had known. My overwhelming feeling was of the irony of life in a world governed by mere chance. Stone had lived carefully, cautiously; when we had gone to sales together in my car I had seen his foot going down on an imaginary brake when I had cornered at speed. He had been obsessed with planning, and brought all of his considerable intelligence to bear on the most tedious details of daily life: but, finally, he had been knocked over by a motor-cycle while walking on a country road where an accident was so rare that it merited a double column in the local paper. He had been thrown twenty feet through the air and smashed against a tree. He had lived for a day in great pain, trying vainly to say something.

I knew few of the faces at the graveside apart from Felix Goldman and some other book dealers. All of them had managed to rake up black coats and hats from somewhere. I felt conspicuous in my light trench coat, too big and bulky. Ann's hand tugged sharply at my arm and I wrenched my thoughts back with a nearly physical movement. We shuffled and filed slowly back along the slushy gravel path. At the narrow gateway there was a hold-up as people hung back elaborately in their determination not to transgress the protocol of the day.

Tassiter was stumping off, his shoulders humped. His daughter's pigtails looked like black wet ropes in the street's gas-light. I ran a few steps and caught them up and pushed half a crown into her hand. 'For sweets,' I explained, but Tassiter pulled her away with a grunt down the street towards the station.

When I got back to the cemetery gate, Margaret and Ann were waiting for me. I got into the first car with them as they seemed to expect me to do so. I sat back with a sigh, and a rather sick feeling, holding the worn corded strap by the door. My head throbbed and my mouth was dry. The luxurious but ancient Daimler limousine sped along silently, the only noise being a faint steady hissing on the wet road.

'What a rotten night,' Ann said, leaning forward. Her tone was casual, just as if we had come out of a cinema. There were no more tears. 'We're going to Mrs White's for a meal,' she added.

I had never heard of Mrs White before. I studied Ann's slightly thickened profile in the street lamp's light. As the car turned a sharp corner Margaret put her hand in mine and left it there. In her soft warm palm there was a tiny screwed-up ball of a handkerchief.

2

THE HOUSE we pulled up at was a small one in a depressed-looking dark row. As we got out there was a buzz of excited voices – other cars had got there before us. Someone rang at the door and we pushed up the path. The house was silent and unlit. No one seemed to be in there but more and more people crowded into the tiny garden. The atmosphere had changed completely in the ten minutes' drive. A large woman banged on the door and called out, 'Jacqueline, Jacqueline!' There was some pushing from behind and a man in front of me was pressed into a damp border. Somewhere in the house a cistern flushed noisily and a front light went on. More laughter. Anyone going down the street would have thought we were a gay theatre party. Goldman hugged my shoulder and whispered in my ear; I could smell gin and old-fashioned cashews. 'I must have a word with you,' he said.

We were propelled through a tiny crowded hall made nearly impassable with coats sticking out from a stand, and into a lounge stuffed with cheap, modern furniture under a glaring light. Margaret and Ann had disappeared upstairs. I knew nobody in the room. My headache had descended heavily and I could feel a pulse in my brow above my left eye. I felt I was taking part in someone else's dream; mine were usually organized differently from this. Someone offered me a plate of ham rolls. This kind of party seemed macabre to me, but then I had not had much experience of them. I decided to relax and let go. Anything could happen as far as I was concerned. I moved to the table, poured myself a double whisky and took a greedy helping of beef sandwiches. From another room I could hear a record of Frank Sinatra singing 'Melancholy Baby'.

'Privately, Robert, we must come to some arrangement.' Goldman had moved in close. The dark, well-cut suits his tailor made for him disguised his heaviness, and he was quite good-looking in a swarthy way, but I found him less congenial than Pettifer, who had an enormous growth on his neck and smelt of mice. Goldman's friendship was always suspect but now it was ludicrous. He was a man I found difficult to handle. He was impervious to any kind of insult, single-minded, and his persistence had worn down my resistance on other deals in the past.

'Look, Felix,' I said, reaching round him for another sandwich, 'Stone hasn't been buried more than an hour. If you think I'm going to start arguing with you now about what's going to happen to his books, you're all wrong. Besides, it's got nothing to do with me.'

'Of course you say that' – Goldman nodded wisely – 'of course. Naturally. You're upset. But as to it not being up to you – well, we know better.' He smiled and laid a thick brown finger beside his nose. His tone became more hurried. 'Don't we? Now look, I can offer you a big cash payment just to have first crack at the coloured stuff. Right now. Two hundred quid for the entrée. A private arrangement!'

Behind his head I could see the top of a small cocktail cabinet cluttered with paper bells and chains. Why had they bothered to take them down before this curious celebration? A fat shiny woman was downing small glasses of port as if they were essential to her existence. Wyse and Handley had come up behind Goldman, and I could understand his anxiety to reach an agreement. If high colour and beery breath could intimidate me, I was sunk.

Wyse came to the point immediately. 'The way I see it, Seldon, you've got your foot in the door. So all right, you get first pick ...' Handley was watching me closely. Goldman appealed to us.

'It's not just the money. Do I need the money?' He stared over the top of my head. 'Do I work just for money?'

The fat woman had finished off the port bottle and had come to the cocktail cabinet to pour from another one. She had the high colour, the glistening skin and noticeable veins of a heavy drinker.

She muttered 'What a day! What rain!' to Goldman, who was not listening. 'It takes a funeral to make you appreciate being alive. You forget your own little worries,' she added. Her philosophy was thrown away on us.

'Sorry,' I said to Wyse. 'I can't begin to discuss it now. Even if it was up to me, nothing can be done in a hurry.'

I started to move away but Handley held my arm. 'Wait! We know you've got the family's interests at heart.' He said this in a funny way but I did not understand the meaning behind the words. 'We know that, Bob, but we'll give her a fair deal. She'll do all right with us.'

Handley was a fairly good liar. No hesitation, and the words came over convincingly. But he had a bad memory, fatal for anyone who wants to lie well over a period of time. When I first met him in 1948 he had told me about his wartime experiences in North Africa; two years afterwards he had confided to me in a beery mood about the five years he spent in the R.A.S.C. stores in Birmingham.

Goldman fingered his heavy gold watch. 'I would sooner work any day buying and selling books at fair prices, than have a thousand pounds given me,' he mused.

'I must go,' I said, shrugging off Handley's hand.

'Best of luck, Seldon,' said Wyse, giving me a bleak smile. He and Handley exchanged blank looks.

From the doorway I could see Margaret and Ann standing together in the room across the small hall. Posed like that I could see that Ann was, physically, a rather poor copy of her sister. Where Margaret was plump, Ann was over the borderline of fatness. Her hair was auburn coloured too, but lacked the richness of Margaret's. They both had such slender legs and small feet that they were inclined to look top-heavy, but in Ann's case this was emphasized by the thickness of her arms.

I looked at my watch. It was just six o'clock. I was undecided what to do. I'd arranged to stay the night at Walker's Hotel in case I could help in any way, but I felt tired, nervy and rather useless. I thought the two sisters would probably talk more easily without me. I felt like getting a late train back to London. Certainly

14

the prospect of an evening in Walker's Hotel was not attractive. A small commercial place, clean and reasonably comfortable, yet the public rooms were dim and full of old-fashioned furniture, and the small lounge was always crowded with commercial travellers yarning about their calls.

'You don't know me,' whispered a nervous-looking little woman with a sharp pointed face and a mop of grey hair like steel-wool, 'but I'm a friend of Ted's, from the north. What a tragedy it was! Do you know what we ought to do? Scrap all those motor-bikes, and the cars. Get back to the old-time peace.'

'Pre-1914, you mean?' I said.

'Yes,' she said, gesturing quickly, 'we can't stand the racket – the pace of machines.'

'It would be a bit difficult to support fifty million people now without cars or lorries on the road,' I said.

'Five million's enough, I should think.' She smiled. 'That's a good number. With space to move about in without being murdered.' I smiled too, then realized she was serious. 'What about the other forty-five million?' I asked.

She ignored my question. A nerve had stopped twitching in her cheek. Her expression was more peaceful, one of quiet fanaticism. 'Five million, not more. Perhaps not as many,' she added doubtfully. She glided off silently to find another supporter for her campaign.

Margaret waved to me, a tiny tentative gesture. I looked questioningly at her as she came into the hall.

She picked out her coat from the crowded rack. 'Will you take me home now, Bob? I'm so tired I can't stand.'

'Sure. But hadn't you better say good-bye?'

'Why? Who to? What's going on here anyway?' Her lips were set petulantly. They were more emphasized by make-up than I remembered before. The atmosphere in the hall was thick with the smell of wet furs and cigarette smoke.

She leaned back heavily as I helped her with her coat, so heavily and with her eyes shut that I thought she might be ill or fainting. But after a shuddering sigh I sensed that she had relaxed a little.

We hesitated on the step in the fresh evening air. The rain had stopped and the sky was clear and bright with the new moon.

Only a few fast high-moving clouds remained. There was still a touch of dampness in the air, with the scent of fir trees which lined the roads leading to the sea. Margaret sighed heavily again as we stepped down. She seemed loath to stay or go.

As we walked down the path she was close to me and I was very conscious of her full, warm body through the thin stuff of her coat. As we went through the gate she put her arm in mine and a kind of shock went through me at the contact. I think we both felt this, and we walked quite a way in silence.

'Is it far?' I asked.

'No, just round the corner. Jacqueline's house backs on to ours,' she explained. 'Did you meet her, Bob? She's the only friend I've made round here. Ted would never have anyone in.'

'Never?' I asked.

'Oh, I know he liked you to come, but that was only because you talked about books. He didn't –' she hesitated and we walked again in silence. When we turned a corner she continued: 'No, Jacqueline is my only real friend.' She said it in a way that made me feel guilty. 'She took charge of everything ... after the hospital.' I hadn't been thinking of Stone just then, but she thought I had. 'Did you really like him, Bob?' she asked.

'Of course. Why?'

'He was a cold man, you know. He really didn't need to be liked. And there wasn't anyone there this afternoon who really cared twopence for him. Or for me, for that matter,' she added defiantly.

This was so obviously untrue that I looked at her quickly. She was staring fixedly ahead with wide eyes, her face strained with a bitter expression. I wondered if she was going to break down and cry at last.

'But that's not true, Margaret. You know it's not. What about Ann?' I said.

'She doesn't care. Oh, she's taken two days off to "cheer me up". But when that's over ... God, how alone we all are, always.'

I did not know where we were. Coming from a strange direction had completely upset my vague knowledge of the area, and I was just following her steps mechanically. But I could sense that we must be getting near the house. She was gripping my arm and her steps were slower and shorter. I did not relish entering the house either.

We stopped at the gate. I had never seen the house completely in darkness before. It looked older and bigger somehow. A large elaborately clipped bush in the centre of a small lawn moved slowly and ominously in a stir of wind. The dark house seemed to be waiting for us. As we went up to the door another evergreen bush brushed my shoulder, its springy leaves spattering drops into my face. This was the bush that I remembered Stone threatened to have chopped down. Now it had outlasted him.

3

It was not really cold in the house but then it was usually overheated. Stone had hated the cold and had spent a lot of money on having an automatic central-heating system installed. We stood quite still for a moment in the hall. The quietness disturbed only by the slow tick of a clock made a curious atmosphere. I knew this was only in my mind, but it was hard to shake off. Margaret shivered and then spoke in an unnaturally loud voice. 'I've got to go upstairs – my clothes are wet. Pour yourself a drink.' She ran up the stairs. 'In there,' she said, pointing down to the study.

The house was stuffed with gadgets. Stone had showed me them all, like the lights that automatically lit when cupboard doors were opened. He had spent a lot of time getting everything exactly as he wanted it.

I poured myself a whisky from the decanter that stood on the heavy polished table and looked along the book-shelves that faced me. For Stone each of the volumes had had so much meaning; I could clearly visualize him opening the case and taking a book down in his large hand, pointing to a phrase with a white, wax-like finger. But from Goldman's point of view the cases were just stuffed with money; my feelings were not much different, and Margaret seemed to be irritated by the books more than anything else. At least it looked as if it would be easy to persuade her to sell them.

With a curious sensation I sat down slowly in the chair behind Stone's desk. There was not much time to search for what I wanted and the moment was inopportune. And I did not know exactly the form of the thing I was looking for. It might be a list or a notebook locked in his desk or poked away in a cupboard. But a large exercise-book seemed more likely, a stout pre-war book neatly filled with his clear, rather childishly rounded writing.

'Ah, that's better.' I had not heard Margaret come down. When I turned she was standing with the door closed, resting against it. Her face was pale but she was smiling faintly. She had changed into a cream, silk dressing-gown; it looked Chinese, a lovely thing with a number of little scenes worked on it in gold and brightly coloured silks. Just below her shoulder a heavy-winged pink bird flew forever across a reedy river and a ramshackle bridge. At her waist two kimonoed lovers were disappearing into a tiny house. Her hair was loose to her shoulders. I had never seen it down before or realized how unfashionably long it was. Her legs were bare and at first I thought that her feet were too, but she was wearing tiny ivory coloured slippers. She held something behind her. Then she brought her hand forward and I could see it was a metal box. She placed it carefully on the table and then put both hands up to her hair, flinging it back from her neck. She stood still and stretched her arms down by her side, breathing slowly and deeply, relaxing in the warmth of the room.

'I'm going to have a drink too.' She raised her arm again and I could see that the gown was cut in eastern fashion with very wide sleeves. She sat down heavily on the couch. 'You know, I shall be depending on you, Bob. Selling all the books. I've got very little apart from them. What does that mean?'

'You've got nothing to worry about in that way,' I said. 'Without going into it carefully I can't be too exact; but there's a lot of money there. Perhaps fifteen or twenty thousand pounds locked up in those cases.'

'Really? As much as that?' she said excitedly, sitting up and staring at the cases as if seeing them for the first time.

'I should say fifteen thousand at least.' As long as Goldman does not handle it for you, I thought.

Her green eyes were wide. 'Oh, we must have another drink on that.' She got up and kneeled round on the couch, stretching out futilely in the direction of the bottle. She could not reach it and knew she could not, but stayed like that with the sleeve falling back from her white smooth arm.

19

I moved towards the decanter and noticed a photograph of Stone on a small table: his level gaze seemed to watch me with subdued amusement. Margaret giggled: she was so different from the person I had known before that I wondered how much she had had to drink already.

'Can you see to it for me, arrange everything about the books?' she asked.

'Of course I can. But surely you knew this stock was valuable? Where did you think the money came from to pay for all this?' I pointed to the thick fitted carpet and gleaming cases which would not have been out of place in the most luxurious Mayfair shop.

'Yes, I knew he made a good living. But he never told me anything. Perhaps twenty thousand? That's a fortune!'

She got up and lifted the box from the table. A pleasant little tune began as she held it close to her. I sat back listening, closing my eyes for a moment. When I opened them Margaret had moved towards me, an absorbed look on her face. I could see her eyes and Stone's photograph both regarding me at once. Her soft full mouth opened and I saw the lighter colour of her inner lip. It looked like an exotic kind of fruit. She sat down again and lifted a foot in the direction of the radiator. As she raised it her slipper came away from her heel and then fell to the floor. She sat still, watching me.

I realized in which direction we were drifting. Within a few hours of Stone's burial I was near to making love to his widow. I shook my head as if to clear it of all my confused feelings, but it was with a half-hearted effort that I made to leave. As I began to get up she put her hand on my sleeve: 'Are you hungry? Shall I get you a meal?'

'No, I took plenty of sandwiches and I can get something at the hotel.'

'Well, sit down for a moment then. I feel much better now. As if some of my troubles had vanished.'

The music box's tinkling tune faltered and stopped with a click. We both held our breath, listening, as if waiting for it to start again. She lay back against my shoulder. As she moved, the dressing-gown, held only by a girdle, parted, and I could see a light green nightdress beneath it. The skin at her neck was completely white, smooth, nacrous. Her breasts were very full, tightly imprisoned by the smooth green material which sharply outlined the hard nipples. Suddenly she turned towards me, putting her right hand round my neck and pulling my face down to hers.

As I kissed her she took my right hand and pushed it under the gown and the narrow strap on her shoulder. Her eyes were shut, the shadowy lids dark and fluttering. I kissed her lips and then the curve of her neck. As I did so she made quiet little noises in my ear. She held my head between her breasts and we lay like that unmoving. All the tension drained away. I forgot Stone, Goldman, everything. We seemed to be alone in the world, suspended, timeless.

There was a small noise somewhere: it seemed to be right in the room. I jerked my head round. But it came from behind the curtains; someone was tapping at the window. Then steps moved along the path. Margaret sprang up: 'Hell – it's Ann! I'd quite forgotten her.'

I went into the hall. The knocking was loud and continuous now. When I opened the door Ann swept past me. 'Why didn't you answer before?' Then she saw Margaret behind me. 'I didn't know where you were – I was worried ...' Slowly she took in our flushed faces and Margaret's appearance. Then she gave a stifled exclamation and ran to the stairs.

'I'm going up right now – and don't worry, I shan't come down.' She turned and shouted at us, her face white and taut with nervous lines. 'Not for anything!'

As she disappeared I turned and suddenly caught sight of my own face in the hall mirror, flushed, stiff and apprehensive. My hair, soaked by the rain, had dried in a kind of black cap. I looked like a sad clown.

'I'm sorry about this,' I said, putting my hand on Margaret's shoulder without any of the passion I had felt only a few minutes before.

'Don't be sorry – don't!' she said, taking hold of the lapels of my raincoat, as I struggled into it. 'I wanted it.' I looked at her without

21

saying anything. 'Oh, you don't understand. He never wanted me in that way. He hardly touched me.'

She looked down. Through the thin gown I could feel her warm body against mine. She bent her head back slightly and I buried my face in the soft curling tendrils on her neck and kissed the warm scented curve there. I felt lost again and had to pull away roughly.

4

I DON'T REMEMBER finding my way back to the hotel. Somehow I was there in the dim hallway with its oddly old-fashioned smell and four ancient stuffed birds in dusty cases. One of the birds was on the point of collapsing; its legs had nearly given way and most of its feathers were on the floor of the case. A commercial traveller I knew slightly saw me through the glass door, pointed and spoke to me in an elaborate dumb show, but I went on through to Hoskins' desk.

Hoskins, a friendly dwarf-like figure who was always on duty there at night, was another relic from the past. They would never get a modern youth to do his thankless, uncomfortable job with half his courtesy. He fitted well behind the desk and in the gloomy alcove, finding letters and keys and writing in a big ledger, but I could not imagine him away from the hotel. Where did he live, I wondered. In my mind he was associated with the period when these tall narrow Victorian buildings had flourished, with bullied skivvies running up from damp basements with cans of hot water. His heavy, rather flat face moved slightly into a look of recognition and he turned the register slowly round in his large dry hands. He spoke in a tired monotonous voice: 'A very rough day, Mr Seldon. Sandbourne doesn't usually let us down so badly. Newspaper and tea in the morning? Do you want to be called late, sir?'

The corners of his mouth twitched in a slow grin and I suspected that there might be lipstick on my face. I stumbled on the first step. I felt drunk, but it wasn't the couple of drinks which had made my hand shake.

Four flights of the steep winding stairs sobered me. This place had always struck me as a fire-trap and I came back to it only as a creature of habit who is loath to try somewhere new which might be worse. I always got the top floor, as I usually arrived without a prior booking, and the fifth flight of stairs was particularly narrow, steep and airless. Going up them, pulling hard on the banister, I was reminded irresistibly of a nightmarish film I had seen starring Peter Lorre some years before. It had shown him as an immigrant to New York who spent his first night there in a dark tenement building: it burnt down in a fire and he was pulled out minus most of his face, and spent the rest of the film wearing a rubber mask.

When the door of the little room was closed behind me I felt as if I was shut in an oven. I went to the small window and pushed my head out into the cold night air. The sky was completely clear and bright: the streets lit by the moon looked unreal and mysterious. The pulse in my forehead had stopped throbbing, but I still felt nervous and under tension. The day had gone on too long for me and too much had happened. I had a wash in the toy-like, awkward hand bowl and lay down on the bed.

It was very odd to think that my present anomalous position really stemmed from and led back to Frederick Lupin, a writer whom I had never known and who had been dead for some forty years. I could not remember when I had first heard of Lupin but I had certainly read one of his books during the war on a beach near Bari, a tattered ex-library copy which a G.I. had lent me. Gradually I had read more of his books, became interested in him and learnt as much as possible of his curious personality and his mainly unhappy life.

Years before I actually met Edward Stone, another book dealer had shown me a Catalogue which Stone had compiled in 1942 of a large Frederick Lupin collection. He had also described in this Catalogue the notorious collection of letters written by Lupin, called the 'Ibiza' letters as they were written from that then little-known Balearic island. My interest in this Catalogue had been one reason why I was glad to make Stone's acquaintance, but he had never been willing to discuss the letters with me. Knowing that he was as much a collector as a dealer, I suspected that it was possible he might not have sold them from the Catalogue and had decided to keep them for himself, but I could not understand why this should prevent him from talking about them.

I had raised the subject several times in oblique ways but had been hedged off: and this obstinacy engendered a curiosity on my part out of all proportion to the interest of knowing the fate of the letters. I knew that he kept a record of the more important collections he had sold, and it seemed that I might now discover what had happened to them. I had a sound financial reason too for investigating the matter, reposing in my pocket in the form of the crumpled cablegram.

My mind was going round and round this in a pointless fashion when I suddenly remembered Margaret. Up to this moment she had faded from my mind completely. I wondered what was happening to me. I regarded myself as far from perfect but with some claims to being considered a human being. Now, within a few hours of a friend's burial, I had made love to his widow and when that had been accomplished my only thought was of a secret that might be uncovered by his death.

I got up and tried to stop thinking by going through various mechanical actions. I took a few things out of my bag and put them in the mothball-smelling drawer, brushed my teeth and undressed. I read a few pages of an old magazine that I found in the wardrobe, and then lay for a long while with my eyes open staring out of the tiny window before I could blot out my thoughts.

I had an old dream with a new variation. Once more I was in the road where I had lived as a child, looking for my house. I went up and down several times: there were numbers 9 and 13, 15 and 17, but our house-number, 11, was not there. Then I thought I saw my father and ran after him calling, but he increased his speed when I had nearly caught up with him.

Suddenly the scene changed and I was back in Italy and we were faced by a machine-gun post. We had brought up a flame-thrower: the concrete box became a mass of flames and tiny blazing figures burst out shrieking. They ran faster and faster, fanning the flames and turning into balls of fire. Someone behind me said, 'They always run', in a dull casual voice. I ran after one of the Germans, trying to catch up with him. He fell and writhed on the ground. When I bent down the flames had vanished. I turned the body over, to find it was not burned at all. It was not a German soldier but Stone, his eyes wide with terror and his mouth open in a soundless cry.

5

I WOKE WITH a start to see that Hoskins was looking closely at me as he put something down beside the bed. He did not say anything and for a minute his blank face looked hostile, his small deformed body twisted over me. There was a fleck of tobacco stuck to his large colourless mouth, his eyes the colour of caramels were half-shut and he was breathing noisily. As he went out of the room I saw the cup of tea and the paper he had brought for me on the table. I realized that in his kind of shy, humble servility he had just not said anything after calling me as I had not greeted him.

I went out of the hotel to find that it had rained hard in the night. The morning was cold, and fine rain still swept along in gusts of wind. I walked with the purpose of getting a view of the sea, but contented myself with the first prospect I came to. From a curious narrow angle I stared down from a shelter at a small section of the dark forbidding waves.

Thinking about my relationship with Stone was like inspecting a wound. Over it guilt was splashed from the incident of the previous night, but beneath the bandage of how I had believed I felt about him there was something I had never probed before. There had been a slight feeling of unease. Had I been wary of his friendship? Or was I now attempting to justify my own behaviour?

I sensed there was something doubly odd in Margaret's attitude. I knew that death and funerals were sometimes supposed to have an erotic effect: I could understand that she might have been carried away in a state of emotional drunkenness. Obviously with her it had not been only sudden physical attraction, overpowering in its intensity, such as I had felt. To do such a thing on the night of Stone's funeral in his room she must have wished to insult or degrade his memory. For what reason? It was particularly puzzling as I had had no idea that their relationship was an unhappy one. Had anyone asked me I should have described their marriage as a fairly good one, though I had certainly never seen any physical demonstrations of tenderness. On the other hand I had not known them to quarrel or heard any backbiting.

The more I thought about Margaret the more enigmatic her behaviour seemed. Instead of phoning I went round to her house. I was so early the newspapers had not been taken in, and she and Ann were still at breakfast. Ann was quite friendly and gave no sign of her feelings about the scene in the hall. The atmosphere was normal: Margaret, apart from one long secret look, seemed to have changed back into the person I had known previously.

I spent an hour or two looking through Stone's papers and his bookshelves, including those in the lounge which had housed his private collection. Ostensibly I was engaged on a preliminary valuation, but I took the opportunity to search for anything relating to the Lupin letters. There was nothing, and I was forced to accept the fact that he had probably sold them to a collector who had asked him to keep the matter confidential. Nor could I find the ledger detailing collections he had sold. I told Margaret that I would have to return to London but would put the valuation for probate into the hands of an expert who specialized in such things. We parted with a friendly handshake: I found it hard to believe that this very slightly matronly figure in a dark-blue wool dress was the passionate woman whose body had been so hungry for my touch just twelve hours before.

In the train going back to London I was lucky with the luncheon and took my time over excellent cauliflower soup, halibut and roast beef. When the coffee came I took the cable form once more from my pocket and smoothed it out on the table. It read: 'WUX TDL LOS ANGELES CALIF 12 13 101 PMP SELDON BOOK WESDO LONDON WILL PAY FIVE HUNDRED POUNDS STERLING FOR LUPIN IBIZA LETTERS FIRM OFFER ORVILLE.'

My assistant, June Collins and I regarded Bernard Orville as a mystery man, and this cable out of the blue – for I had previously no idea that he was interested in Lupin – was just another reason for confirming our viewpoint. Book collectors are often eccentrics: their personalities are salty, their tastes individual and unusual. After years of dealing in rare books and catering to customers' whims I considered myself accustomed to off-beat requests and odd behaviour, but Orville was just a little more mysterious and unpredictable than most.

He had first walked into my office about three years before, dressed in a sober, perfectly cut suit of dark brown flannel, with a heavy cream shantung shirt and a dark brown silk tie. He had been similarly dressed on each of his other, infrequent visits. He was a large, rather flabby man, always slightly tanned and immaculately groomed, with a limp handshake and light grey eyes that avoided looking directly at you.

The first time he had called at my office he had picked out an edition of *Les Chants du Maldoror* illustrated by Salvador Dali, priced at eighty pounds, and three other fairly expensive books, in a diffident casual manner, and paid for them in new five-pound notes. He had discussed the Dali drawings in a curious off-hand way which I found was habitual. His interest in books seemed perfunctory despite the fact that he appeared to have a large collection. His first purchase remained with us for three months until he sent a messenger to take the books to the Savoy.

From time to time he would phone and inquire in a very quiet melodious voice whether I had anything 'in his line'. I had only the vaguest idea of the kind of books likely to interest him but tentatively offered anything unusual on Surrealism, black humour, and the generally morbid productions of a little-known Paris private press. Our relationship was a strictly commercial one and I was glad that it was for a number of reasons: mainly because I had a feeling that he was always laughing at me somewhere deep down, no matter how seriously he spoke. His habitually grave and formal manner appeared to cover a sardonic, nihilistic attitude.

His enthusiasms were short-lived and his telephoned communications were complicated. Invariably he would phone from a bar, in Venice, Berlin or Paris, often with the row of a party in the background, and operators would butt in to add to the confusion of the various noises: these difficulties seemed to please rather than annoy him. He did not mind how often we got cut off and sometimes I suspected he was doing it to add to the general bizarre effect. One call from Amsterdam, which June had to handle, proceeded quite reasonably until a third party, a Chinese with a high-pitched laugh, had joined in.

But these eccentricities were more than offset by the fact that he always paid spot cash for anything he bought from me, and I considered him a reasonably good customer. He had not given us an American address and we had no way of getting in touch with him, but I felt sure that he would be following up this cable and that the offer of five hundred pounds was a serious one if I could find the letters quickly.

6

WHEN I GOT back to my flat in Ealing the streets were deserted beneath a grey mist of fine rain. It was a Sunday of the blankest possible kind. The pleasures of being a bachelor were at their lowest ebb. The flat was dusty, cold and unwelcoming. It was not a home but just three rooms with some meaningless objects where I was accustomed to eat and sleep. The few things in my tiny larder looked completely unrelated to food. As I stared round the living-room, the pictures I had taken time to collect now seemed absolutely pointless: I could not understand the impulse that had led me to bother with them.

I did not want to stay in and yet had no desire to go out. I lay on a couch for a while and stared blankly at the wall. Then I made some coffee and brooded over Stone's Catalogue as if it was a clue which might possibly lead me to Orville's five hundred pounds.

The Catalogue was a thin pamphlet bound in faded green wrappers with rusty staples. It was dated 'Winter, 1942. A Catalogue of Rare Books including a complete collection of the works of Frederick Lupin and an important series of letters.' The letters were described at length at the end of the Catalogue:

Frederick S. Lupin (1870–1916). Author of *Initiate*, 1892; *Pasquinade*, 1900, etc. A collection of thirty original letters written to 'Paolo' from Ibiza, 1914–16. Though unpublished these letters have become well known in literary circles. They give a fantastic but probably faithful picture of the author's last years which he spent wandering through S.W. France and Spain, finally settling in a 'Castle' near Ibiza in the most southerly of the Balearic Islands.

To quote briefly from these letters would do them an in-justice, but it can be said that the lyrical passages compare with his descriptions of the Camargue and Provence generally, to be found in his last published work, *Troubador* (1915). There are vivid descriptions of his day-to-day life of the kind that figures in *A Goat's Paradise* (1910), together with vitriolic attacks on contemporaries including many well-known figures in the literary and publishing world of the time. There are also appeals for money. Some of the letters contain hints of the perverted debauchery with which Lupin ruined his own life and many others.

The letters are in their appearance alone works of art. Each one is carefully set out and beautifully written in hands of varying size on many different kinds of paper. One begging note is in the form of a medieval manuscript on a folio page of white, Tuscan, hand-made paper. The writing is in jet-black ink with a drawing of a hog rooting for acorns surrounding the capital D. Many of the other letters include small drawings, including one of his 'Castle'. The letters have been mounted on uniform sheets of stiff paper and bound in a volume of levant morocco. Price: £200.

There were lots of things about Lupin that did not appeal to me. I did not share his enthusiasm for the Medieval period, Roman Catholicism and ultra-Toryism, or his interest in the Occult. I had no sympathy with his homosexuality or his hatred of women. I found his spitefulness irritating. But his courage fascinated me. Indeed, this aspect of his character became quite an obsession with me as I found out more about him.

For most of his life Lupin was shabby, poor and friendless. He was often hungry and cold, and sometimes in a degrading position for anyone so sensitive. He was small and ugly, with a livid scar on his cheek: he was shy and stammered badly. But his courage was a constant factor in his life and apparent from all accounts. Wilkinson, who financed his first trip to Languedoc and was badly repaid by being caricatured as the 'fat, white, ineffectual Wilkie …', referred to 'his boundless spirit'. And Lupin's obituary by Father Sanders quoted some apposite lines from a poem by John Davidson. 'His heart was worn and sore':

At the swoop of death
He sang aloud in the dark
And touched the heart of the world.

I had first realized that I was a coward in 1939. I was on holiday in the South of France just before the outbreak of war, and spent all my time with an international group of youngsters who were staying at the Provençal Hotel in Juan-les-Pins. There was a curious, exciting atmosphere: single strands of barbed wire were being carelessly looped up by Colonial soldiers along the beaches; the hotel staff continually diminished as waiters were mobilized; our parents sat round discussing the prospect of war while others prudently made arrangements to leave. Most of the under-twenty group were left to themselves, feckless, carefree. We secretly opened and monopolized the shut-down water-ski bar, helped ourselves to unlimited gin and tonics, danced in bathing costumes to old Benny Goodman and Arty Shaw records.

There was a German boy called Rudiger von Entlow who was surrounded by mystery as we expected him to be recalled to the Fatherland, but he and his father seemed unconcerned by the headlines. Rudiger had an enormous Mercedes open tourer: a wealthy Turkish boy drove an old green Bentley racing car. We all crowded into these and drove along the coast roads at reckless speed.

One day we stopped at a deserted headland for a bathe. It was a fascinating place, surrounded by steep smooth rocks and deep clear pools. Rudiger, an American girl called Dolores Ross and I went off exploring and found a dark shady gorge where the sea swirled in to form a pool some twenty feet beneath us. As we peered down Dolores slipped. She fell back under the waves and turned over. Her face was white apart from a small purple bruise on her forehead. Then she disappeared under a flat shelf of rock which covered the entrance to the open sea. I stood and watched: the pool was so narrow, the rocks so steep and threatening. But von Entlow jumped down without hesitation, apparently without a thought for the danger, and swam after her. Within a few minutes he was helping her back to the side of the headland.

No one commented on my failure to do anything. I could even justify it to myself. Rudiger was a much stronger swimmer: there was no point in us both jumping into the narrow channel. But for years afterwards I would dream of that strangely cool and dark place, hidden from the brilliant sun, with the girl's body turning over curiously slowly so that one could see her eyes were closed, while I stood by in the grip of a useless panic. Some memories live on in us like wounds.

7

I REVISITED THE South of France as soon as I could after the war, in 1949. The rare book business I had started after my demobilization in 1946 had done well. I stayed in Juan again. As I lay on the *plage* I was obsessed by all the changes brought about in ten years. It seemed a completely different world. What had happened to Dolores, to the Turkish boy, whose name I could not remember, to the von Entlows, who had been taken away by the gendarmes on the day war was declared?

For a while I luxuriated in a pleasant melancholy and indulged my penchant for such nostalgic thoughts. A few days were enough to make me realize how impossible it is to recapture anything of the past. So to give my trip some object I decided to leave Juan-les-Pins and try to trace Lupin's trail from France to Spain which he described so well in *Troubador*.

I inquired at many of the inns he mentioned in the hope that someone might remember him. No one in France had heard of him, but one old woman who owned a *pension* at Banyuls tried her best to provide memories of an eccentric visitor some thirty odd years before. She nodded wisely: 'Oui. Monsieur Lupin. Un écrivain, disiez-vous. Ah oui, je m'en souviens très bien. Un peu excentrique peut-être. Mais charmant, charmant. Grand. Bien fait de sa personne. Il buvait trop. Et souvent après les femmes ...'

She had rambled on and in the end had given me a fairly interesting picture of this completely imaginary character. Sitting at a chipped green metal table on a pine-sheltered terrace, I had been content to listen and pay for her glasses of the cheap local wine and watch her gestures and grimaces. Her attention to my feigned reactions and her improvisations were excellent. And from my seat I could see some small girls absorbed with a delightful seriousness in dancing a *sardane*, a favourite Catalan dance, just the kind of scene that Lupin would have come across in this same place.

From Banyuls I passed through Estaings, managing to combine the Lupin itinerary with seeing the annual Procession of St Fleuret. But I was not able to find anyone there, or in two Costa Brava villages, who recalled him.

When I at last arrived in Ibiza it was different. A kind of excitement had grown in me during the trip, and as soon as I saw the island I realized why it had been journey's end for Lupin and therefore for me in my quest. There were so many attractions for him: the colour, heat and light (light of an unique, brilliant, shimmering quality); the transparent sea; the remoteness from England where he had been so miserable and his work rejected; but mainly the atmosphere of the place. The sad air of the people, resigned to their poverty and yet proud, was sympathetic to him. He had translated some of the Arabic-Andalusian *casidas* and the *cante jondo*, the passionate songs of the Andalusian gypsies, that strange race which forms the last reservoir of the Moorish influence in Europe. In Ibiza Lupin had found the kind of life he had always wanted, and he had been accepted there.

One of the first group I questioned, an old fisherman, remembered him well. I had a drink with this man in a café of abject poverty. There was a background of shouting in the next room and faintly somewhere I could also hear a very old, feeble voice repeating endlessly, 'Aiou Jesu. Jesu.'

But the old salt's firm voice captured my attention. 'El capitan de navio. Con una cicatrix? I ho! un gran nadador – y pescador. Le apreciabamos mucho ...' He described Lupin's semi-naval clothes: the rough, blue serge trousers and white roll-necked pullover and peaked cap. His fantastic swimming feats and the fact that he had learnt to fish as well as the natives with a *rai*, a circular net to catch the *saupes* that swam in that part of the Mediterranean, had impressed the fisherman deeply. And he remembered Lupin's agility when they stalked *merou* and fat *merluzas* in the deep pools at night by torchlight with a *fitora*, a long-hafted double-headed trident.

Another old woman remembered him in Santa Eulalia, remembered particularly his penchant for dressing up on occasions, the flowing red robe he sometimes wore and his silver and scarab rings. From there he had gone to his final home, a few miles along the coast. And I followed him there, with a lovely doe-eyed girl of seventeen, her violet petticoats hitched carelessly around her knees, as a guide.

We approached Lupin's 'Castle' through a landscape of unusual beauty. We passed deserted farm houses with pink and white walls five feet thick; and misshapen fig trees which seemed to moan because of the doves hidden in their branches. Salt flats and red sand shimmered in the dazzling white light. Lizards slithered from our path, but a small brightly coloured bird followed us at a safe distance. The girl walked easily and apparently tirelessly through the coarse grass, over stones and then into an area of desolate sandhills. I wondered how much longer I could keep up the pace in the terrific heat when she suddenly pointed to the 'Castle', a tower springing from the beach. She told me it was reputed to have been built in the last century for a nameless eccentric lady. It was quite derelict. As we approached, birds took off from the crumbling top and I could see a fine spray of sand blowing from the window spaces.

Juanita squatted on the sand. Her guiding mission was over and she did not want to enter the place. She had carried a frying-pan and a string bag, and she commenced to make a fire and cook some fish for our lunch. I had brought a large flask of the local pink wine made from Roman grapes.

The tower door was shut fast and grown over with blue convolvulus. When I tried the door a cloud of flies buzzed round my head, the old lock gave under the weight of my shoulder and I stumbled into the comparatively cool flag-stoned hall. An armorial shield and the motto 'Mihi sufficit' was painted on the wall. I wondered if Lupin had been guilty of flaunting this hollow tag, or whether it was a relic of the original owner. As I went up the sand-blown shallow steps I remembered Lupin's description of the place as it had been, and faintly hoped that I might find something left behind from his tenancy. After his death some of his belongings had been parcelled up and sent to the British Consul in Barcelona, but such arrangements would inevitably be haphazard.

Lupin's sexual non-conformity had been suppressed while he was in Ibiza, but it was possible that a rumour of the incident in Barcelona, 'un escandalo publico' which had led to him leaving the city, had finally reached the people of Santa Eulalia. For this reason or some other now lost in the past the tower had been shunned for many years after his death. Then it had been inhabited briefly by a fisherman's family, and a band of Anarchists had camped there for a few weeks in 1936 after the outbreak of the Civil War.

I searched the rooms carefully, but there was only dry red sand and the mummified bodies of lizards. From the parapet I looked down to see Juanita's blue-black hair divided in half by its straight white parting. A delicious smell of fried fish and olives drifted up to me.

I had had only a slight hope of finding anything material to show for my literary pilgrimage; I had not been naïve enough to expect manuscripts to remain there through the years. We ate the fish and home-cured ham and mulberries sitting in the shade of the tower. Afterwards the girl began to sing, a sad ululating song – her voice had an untutored but moving tone. I sat listening to her and the sea wind, smelling salt odours mixed with the heavy sweet smell of the locust beans. I was under the spell of Ibiza as Lupin had been – my quest there had ended.

8

THE MONDAY after the funeral, following that depressing, nostalgia-ridden weekend, did not start off well either. When I got to my office I found J. K. Saunders was there, telling my assistant his Henry Stevens story: I had heard it two or three times before but he told it well and she was enthralled. For him it was more than a story – it was a kind of terrible lesson about the nature of life. They barely acknowledged my entrance. June's eyes were wide open. Saunders' hands moved vigorously to demonstrate his point: 'Stevens was all the rage for a time. He was like – well, no poet now would be so popular. He was like ...' Saunders' eyes roamed round the office as if he might find a comparison there. 'Well, he was a kind of Rupert Brooke and Ivor Novello rolled into one. His poetry sold like hot cakes. He couldn't do wrong for a bit. The critics praised everything he wrote.'

Saunders paused and gestured as if in dismissal. 'Then something went wrong. His work didn't change much, but suddenly the public dropped him, and the same critics began to tear his work apart ...'

I looked at the scanty mail on my desk. There were two catalogues, two circulars, and a letter from a lunatic lady in Hollywood offering to sell me a 'St Michael lucky piece'. There was also a rather curt letter from my bank manager asking me to see him.

Saunders smiled cynically as he began to recount the final stages of the Stevens story, but I knew the force and meaning it had for him. A successful stockbroker, Saunders had literary leanings but no talent. He sublimated this interest by collecting books and manuscripts. At times he spent a good deal, occasionally perhaps more than he could afford. In his more sober moments he worried about this extravagance. The stories he told about indigent artists and authors were really self-lectures, to restrain his impulses.

'He went right downhill – lived in abject poverty: destitute, a man like that!' As Saunders continued I could hear more definitely his subdued Lancashire accent; it was as if facing these facts brought out his own basically tough attitude to life. The end came one night in 1916 – aye, '16 I think it was. Stevens died in a dirty attic. His friend was penniless and didn't know what to do. In the end he put the body in a wheelbarrow to take him round to the mortuary. As he was going down the street in the black-out, a policeman challenged him and he ran along pushing the barrow until the body fell out. That was the end of Henry Stevens – poet and playwright.'

Saunders relapsed into silence. June went to make some coffee and I tried to get a little business going by phoning Pennington and asking him to value the Stone collection for me. Pennington was not much of a business man but on the value of books he was first-rate, a walking reference library. Perhaps rather simple outside the narrow world of book auction prices, but absolutely dependable. I stressed the fact that the valuation was to be disclosed only to me and Mrs Stone. Pennington was just right for the job. He was small, fat, bald and incorruptible.

I felt low: it seemed certain that Saunders would not buy anything; he never did after telling one of his salutary stories about the way of the world. He went along the shelves tentatively pulling books out and edging them in again. At the back of his mind was the awe-inspiring lesson. I tore up the Californian lucky letter; then I went round to the Bank and explained that I had sold my car, had cut my overheads to a minimum, and that I had reason to think business would soon pick up.

After a quick early lunch of two smoked salmon sandwiches I went back to the office and brooded on the stock staring at me. I hated most of the books as they had been there so long. And I felt much the same about the room and the view. I had known that it was essential to get a place within a taxi ride of non-ambulatory Americans staying at the Ritz and the Savoy. I had succeeded but only just. My office was too high ('No elevator!'

they exclaimed), too small, and it faced the wrong way. The Mayfair address sounded all right but most people were disappointed when they finally got there. And usually they were too tired to do anything but sit in my one expensive easy chair and get their breath back.

I had just mentally raised the amount I must make out of the Stone deal for the third time when I heard June's gay clicking steps. She was never depressed. She had an allowance from her family and the wages I paid her were not really important. That is the bane of anyone like myself who cannot offer enough money to get an intelligent and hardworking girl, and has to settle for someone who likes 'to work among books', who has four or five incoming telephone calls a day and sometimes a visit from amused debutante friends who want to view a rare book dealer in his natural surroundings.

I looked at my watch. If she had gone off at the usual time she was very late. I considered mentioning this as she burst in with a bounce.

'Wonderful news!' she exclaimed.

I lay back and waited for it. Nothing could be too wonderful for me.

'Yes, really. I sold Mr Saunders *the* Missal!'

I jumped up. This was good news. The medieval manuscript she meant was a very nice thing, but we had had it much too long.

'How much?' I asked. 'Did you come down on the price?'

'The marked price – nett,' she replied triumphantly. 'Two hundred and seventy-five pounds. His cheque will be in the post tonight. I was going to leave a note on your desk but I thought it would be nice to tell you.'

She seemed really pleased. I decided to look out for a present for her as a kind of unofficial commission. I went and stared at the place the Missal had occupied in the case. I could hardly believe that it was gone; it had taken on a permanent look. Saunders must have seen it a dozen times.

'One other bit of news – but not in that class. Mr Hayter phoned. He wants to meet you this afternoon. Three-thirty. The middle of Westminster Bridge.' She said this as if such appointments were common enough, but she could not really cope with Charlie Hayter. Nor could I for that matter, but I tried hard.

I felt I could afford a taxi to Westminster Bridge but did not take one. I would not want to ask the driver to drop me on the middle of the bridge and anyway it was a fine bright day for a walk. Hayter's mysterious assignation had not really surprised me. I could say that without any attempt at sophistication. Once, for reasons of his own, he had arranged to meet me beside Eros. I had been there on time and had seen him alight at the end of Regent Street. He had come forward as if to cross to the island in the road, then turned tail and jumped on a bus going down Piccadilly. This thwarted meeting had never been mentioned between us, but I was unlikely to forget it.

Hayter ran the Bon Ton Literary & Publicity Agency, for what that meant. Actually he existed on the seediest and furthest edge of the quasi-literary world, doing practically anything for a pound or two. In the Welfare State his 'Agency' was obviously an anachronism for he could have earned more money in a factory. He clung desperately to the Bon Ton which had had some minor success in the 1930's but now existed in name only. He had some elaborate letter-headings left over from his first business address, he used the royal 'we' with regard to the Agency's achievements and plans, and that was all. I had known him over a period of years during which he had sunk steadily. Meeting him at intervals was like seeing a twentieth-century version of Hogarth's *Rake's Progress*. Not that there was much of the rake about Hayter, apart from drink. I understood that before the war he had been in prison for a short stretch. That seemed to be the reason for his obsession with the police. He imagined that he was constantly under observation. If he was occasionally, then it was only due to his fantastically nervous manner and not because he was suspected of anything serious.

When I first met him he had a small office in the Strand. High up, of course, but otherwise quite pleasant. He had spoiled the good impression by greeting me from behind a desk on which were piled a number of tins of food, some partly opened. He had tried to sell me a collection of highly personal letters from minor authors addressed to him. I was not too keen about the idea but he had made it very plain that he needed the money badly. The next time I saw him he had left the Strand office and was carrying on a vendetta with his former landlord from a basement flat in the Edgware Road. He looked grubby and hungry but still fairly presentable. He had been wearing a good suit and a pink shirt but was without collar or tie. As I left he handed me a short libellous note which he wanted me to pin on the door of his previous office.

On the last occasion when we had a straightforward meeting, I mean one in which I visited his business premises, he gave me an address in Clerkenwell. When I got there a frowsy looking woman in a flannel nightdress opened the front door, led me through a dark passage, pointed to another door and then went back to bed. Hayter's room behind her flat was small with a tiny window high up in the wall and practically airless. He was unshaven and looked ill. I gave him what he asked for a Dylan Thomas manuscript poem, which looked as if it had been through every pub in London on its strange journey, and escaped as quickly as I could.

9

HIGH ABOVE the bridge seagulls wheeled indifferently in the pale
January sunlight as I walked to and fro waiting for Hayter. There
was a cold wind blowing in from the Channel; the air was keen
and clear; I watched a few lavender and pink-edged clouds changing
shape and chasing quickly across the sky. I breathed in deeply
the salt-tasting air and sniffed appreciatively the distinctive blend
of sea and river smells, and was conscious of enjoyment (free
from guilt) for the first time in many weeks. The previous time
had been two months or so before Christmas when Stone and I
had been to an auction together near Bristol. After it was over we
had journeyed along the Severn and stopped at a village pub. There
we had had a simple but delicious lunch of fresh salmon
sandwiches and glasses of Chablis on a stone terrace overlooking
the river.

For an hour or so we had watched two tiny figures patiently
fishing with a net between some rocks. The late autumnal river
edged by bare trees had an austere beauty: the whole scene had a
timeless quality. There Stone had dropped his usual reticence
and told me an amusing story about his childhood; now he had
been battered to death; there had been a brief notice about him in
the booksellers' trade journal, a longer one in the Sandbourne
paper. His books would soon be dispersed and probably his house
would be sold. His wife seemed all too willing to forget him. His
life had been fairly successful in a way, yet all that remained to
show for it was a file of catalogues. Soon it would be just as if he
had never existed. I looked down on the dark swirling river beneath
the bridge. A pink paper hat floated giddily along and then dipped
suddenly and disappeared.

I looked up to see Hayter jump off a bus going to Black-heath. He landed unsteadily and nearly went down on one knee. He looked round very carefully and then came up to me but did not stop. 'Let's get off this frigging place,' he said as he went past.

I obeyed but looked round as I did so. There was no one in sight. Only a helicopter could have us under observation, or someone with a strong telescope on Big Ben. I followed him back across the bridge to the Westminster station side. 'Where are we going?' I asked mildly. It was no use trying to influence his involved plans.

He flicked me with a cunning glance. 'Teashop. We'll have a quick cup if that's all right, and I'll show you – discuss a business proposition. Got some cash?' he asked.

I nodded – I knew how he felt about cheques. The only form of payment that pleased him was a series of tired-looking pound notes. He was wearing a thick navy overcoat, but beneath the prosperous hem there were frayed light grey trousers and very scuffed old brown shoes. His shirt was khaki with a matching tie. He had shaved erratically and left a nasty flat cut on his left cheek beneath a few long hairs, while a piece of toilet paper staunched another one bobbing up and down near his Adam's Apple.

I got my cup of tea quickly at the self-service counter and waited to pay by the cashier, but he took a long time deciding what to eat. Indeed he hovered so long that we caused a hold-up and I visualized starting off this dubious meeting with a bit of trouble. However, the girls behind the counter eyed him warily and people in the queue behind him waited patiently and quietly. His movements as always were uncertain and he replaced some dishes. But eventually he was seated behind a plate of prunes, tea, two buns, a small section of cheese and a helping of apple sauce.

He eyed these things with considerable satisfaction but made no move to eat them. I wondered how hungry he was. 'You don't like people but you feel sorry for them,' my friend Ben Meyer had acutely told me.

Before reaching for a plate Hayter tugged out a small envelope from an inner pocket. He laid this in front of me. It was an ordinary manilla envelope of the type used for sending out business receipts. There was nothing on it but a few fingermarks. I made no move to pick it up. Hayter took a spoonful of cold apple. His left forefinger came down heavily on the envelope. 'Nothing much in it but I think it will interest you. Worth a quid?'

'Yes,' I said firmly and perhaps a shade too quickly to satisfy his nearly Oriental taste for bargaining.

I passed him the note and opened the envelope. It contained a rather large business card, fancily set out: 'Mr Stephen Winfrith Tennant, 4 Chain Court, Old Kent Road, London, S.E. Fine printing.' I held the card in my hand reflectively. It meant nothing at all to me but I knew that an explanation would follow in Hayter's own time. From our various 'deals' I knew how independent and prickly he was. One of his many idiosyncrasies was that he must appear to dictate the procedure of business. I saw he was playing an elaborate game with a bun which he had cut into a number of small pieces, arranged in a line and proceeded to pop into his mouth as if he was punishing them.

Another envelope appeared from somewhere in the bulky coat. 'You don't know whether you're pleased with that one. But this one explains it. Thirty bob?'

I nodded and took out the money. The Missal had cost me £150 two years before and it had been marked down at a stock-taking since then. I had made a good profit; I felt leisurely and quite prepared to spend some time and a little cash with Hayter. Something would come out of it.

Hayter leaned forward again. He had been spared nothing – his teeth and breath were bad. 'I don't think you will be disappointed,' he said.

I was far from disappointed. The larger envelope contained a quarto sheet of thick, deckle-edged paper folded in half. It was a prospectus, set in an elegant italic type but unevenly printed.

Spring 1943. THE PETRONIUS PRESS announces the publication by subscription only, of *The Last Letters* of Frederick Lupin. The complete unexpurgated text printed from the original holographs. Edition of 100 copies

only on antique paper bound in Italian decorated
boards. Price £3 3. 0. Available in September from
The Petronius Press, 15 Garsington Street, W.C.1.

The whole thing was a puzzle to me. I was sure the book had
not been printed as I would certainly have heard of it if it existed.
'The last letters' and 'unexpurgated text' pointed to it being an
edition of the 'Ibiza' letters.

Hayter pointed to the prospectus. 'Don't know or can't remember
anything about the Petronius Press,' he said, 'but I do know who
printed this.' He showed me a small engraving on the back, a
wood-cut of a cornucopia. 'That's Tennant's imprint all right. He
once did a book of poems for a client of mine. But I had forgotten
all about him and this thing, then Handley was saying in Sotheby's
about you being very interested in Lupin and I came across it
among some other old papers. Not published, you know. See here,
that's my writing. I've pencilled "not issued" on it. But I can't
remember anything about it. Too long ago.'

'1943. Antique paper, Italian decorated boards: funny how they
were able to get such things then,' I said.

'Queer time to be doing a book like that at all,' Hayter agreed.
'But old Tennant was always an invalid and wouldn't have been
called up or anything like that.'

'1943 – when the Russians were on the Dnieper and the U.S.
Marines were at Tarawa.'

'Were you fighting overseas then?' Hayter asked.

I remembered myself sitting in terror's cold grip in a large 'Gin
Palace' wireless van, listening as shells hurtled high overhead.
'Yes, I was abroad.'

Hayter pointed to the remaining prunes and tea. 'I'm going to
take my time over these. Shouldn't wait for me.' He hesitated.
'Don't bank too much on that card. Tennant might well be dead.
Always ill on and off when I knew him. Don't bother to wait.'

He repeated this admonition as if he were used to people leaving
him immediately a 'transaction' was finished. I was tempted to
sit down again. My financial status being so shaky and my ability
sketchy, I was well aware how narrow a margin really separated

me from Hayter's position. My teeth were in better shape but they could fall out, and I would not fit in to a factory job any better than he would. People accepted the front I put up – my clothes were good and until a week before Christmas I had owned a Mercedes car; but I knew my true position and had quite a lot of fellow feeling for Hayter spinning out his meal in the comparative warmth and brightness of the teashop. I wondered how he spent his evenings, what he did on Sundays when there was no chance of any odd deals and all offices and shops were shut.

As I went out of the door I looked back at him again, hunched over the table. He was really alone, much more so than Margaret would be for years to come, but he never complained, never said a word about himself; from his attitude it seemed that he presumed his personal problems were of no interest to anyone else.

10

I HAD A nasty shock just after leaving Hayter. A policeman had given me explicit instructions how to find Chain Court, and I was repeating them to myself – 'St George's Road, Elephant, New Kent Road, Old Kent Road, then second turning on the left after Dunton Road' – when I came level with the last car in a queue at some traffic lights. It was a black Rolls-Royce: in the back, looking out on my side with a bored expression, was Edward Stone. He was dressed in clothes quite unlike those he usually wore, a black overcoat, homburg hat, silver-grey tie. But I knew his pale face, the wide forehead, the deep lines going down from the corners of his mouth. He looked right through me as though I did not exist. Without thinking I moved into the kerb, shouting out something wildly. As I did so the lights changed to green and the cars moved off. The man in the limousine turned round and stared at me in mild surprise. I was convinced that the expressionless, dissembling mask was Stone's. Not dead but drugged, the thought came into my mind, and I noticed a young girl passing by looked at me strangely – I wondered if I had said this out loud.

I must have circumnavigated the Elephant and Castle mechanically because without noticing the intervening streets I was suddenly confronted by the plaque for Dunton Road. The walk through these busy lamp-lit streets had a nightmarish quality: I felt as if I was looking over the shoulder of the man who looked for Chain Court. I was bewildered by my encounter, so much so that for a moment everything seemed unreal, had a deadened quality as if I were experiencing it at second hand.

Chain Court was a small cul-de-sac, a gloomy place lit by only one gas lamp at the end. No. 1 was a newsagent's with no light showing and presumably closed. Nos. 2 and 3 were derelict, their fronts closed by long grimy planks of wood battened across them. The window of No. 4 was lit partly by the street lamp and also by a rather feeble electric light under a parchment shade standing among piles of assorted bric-à-brac. The lettering on the façade read 'The Jewel Shop'.

There was a lot of jewellery on display with two large white plates full of bracelets and necklaces and a number of small boxes containing rings and brooches, but there were also cigar-boxes full of medals, some stamp albums, small statues, a Worcester bowl, a Victorian doll in a broken glass case, an antique camera on a stand. The display was of such variety and mixed quality, being flanked by two interesting small Dutch oil paintings on panels, that I automatically spent some time searching to see if there was anything that I could buy. It was the kind of shop that I would rate as a possible source of supply for the odd book or autograph letter and enter, if I had encountered it in my professional travels.

I had been in scores of antique shops but I could not remember seeing one in which valuable items were so mixed with completely valueless things. Carved wood brackets and charming mirror-sconces, presumably Venetian, stood by a shoe-box full of old spectacles. Two large Liverpool shell-dishes and some ivy-leaf pickle-trays were half-hidden by a pile of worthless 'Cries of London' framed prints. I was fascinated by the mind behind the shop, the character of a person who could acquire a fine chest of coloured lacquer and cover its top with a display of match-box labels.

It was not easy to see into the interior as there were so many things hanging from the ceiling, and there was only a narrow path cleared between odd pieces of furniture from the front door to a counter where I could just make out that two people were seated. I had noticed some things I might possibly buy as a present for June: a silver bracelet with filigree decoration and a tiny gold pencil. They provided me with an excuse to go in. As the address was now a shop I felt that Hayter was probably right in presuming that Tennant was dead, but it was possible that the owner could confirm this.

When I opened the door I could see that the man sitting on a high stool on my side of the counter was a clergyman, plump and rather sleek. He was undressing an antique doll and had just removed some faded lace under-garment. The other man moved quickly and rather aggressively round till he could see me better and then shouted in a high, irritable voice, 'I say, shut the door, old lad, and come in properly if you're going to.'

He was wearing a bottle-green corduroy jacket, dirty yellow corduroy trousers, and a dark blue shirt with a Paisley-patterned tie on a white background. As he pointed I could see that his nails were very long and the one on his forefinger had grown like a tiny penknife blade.

'I'm looking for a Mr Tennant.'

'Then you've found him, dear boy. What luck!' He simpered and ducked his head in a quick bow, showing a lot of greasy, carefully waved hair.

'Mr Hayter said you might be able to ...'

'Hayter?' he interrupted in an aggrieved tone. 'Hayter, Hayter, now who's he?' He did not give me time to reply to this question but went on, 'No one of much consequence, I think. At least, he doesn't loom too large on the horizon just at present. Hayter – let me think. No, you have me puzzled ...' He gave me a very suspicious look. 'Don't know any Hayter, old lad.'

The clergyman looked rather uneasy. He had stopped fingering the doll and was pulling at one of his large pink ears apprehensively.

The clergyman and Tennant exchanged quick glances. Suddenly I had the feeling that they suspected, for some odd reason, that I was from the police. I hastened to reassure them. 'Hayter once had something to do with a book you printed. In fact you printed it for him, or for one of his customers.'

'No, not me. Never printed anything in my life.' Tennant was still regarding me suspiciously, with his head on one side. He examined my shoes, raincoat and tie as if looking for some essential clue.

'I'm a book-dealer,' I said, 'and Hayter said you could tell me something about the Petronius Press. It's old history to you now, but weren't you printing in the war, about 1943?'

'Oh, a dealer,' he said, 'like me. Oh, we must help someone in the trade as it were.' He still hesitated. Then he poked his finger forward to touch my arm as if to identify me. The look of apprehension cleared. 'You want my brother Stephen,' he said simply. 'I'm Selwyn Tennant.'

'He's not here?' I asked.

'Oh, he's here and not here, if you know what I mean. This is his address but he's not what you might call readily available.'

I pulled out the Petronius Press leaflet and showed him the fleuron on the back. 'Hayter said that was your brother's imprint.'

'Yes, it was – and somewhere,' he said, 'somewhere far away a tiny bell is tinkling. I have a vague – but very – recollection of Mr Petronius' Press.' He winked reassuringly at the clergyman. 'Come,' he addressed me, 'come upstairs and meet Stephen.'

We went through faded green baize curtains and then up some dark stairs.

'Sorry I was so very dim just then. But one gets some odd callers at times. People, you know, who can be troublesome, or try to be. This business attracts' – he turned and looked frankly down at me – 'terrible NUTS and one has to be careful.'

It was cold and damp upstairs; the corridor was dimly lit and faint smells of dust and cooking were trapped there. He paused outside the door. 'If Stephen is asleep we can't wake him, but you can try a question if not. He may be able to help you.' He sounded very doubtful and added a rider. 'But unlikely, he's been so ill and now I'm afraid ...' He tapped his forehead.

In the room lit only by a small bedside lamp there was an overwhelming smell of antiseptic. Tennant went to the bedside and peered at the head on the pillow. I did not approach but could just see the sallow forehead with a piece of pink lint on it.

'Don't bother – don't think of disturbing him, it's not that important,' I whispered urgently.

'No luck,' he said, and followed me out quickly. 'Come to think of it, there's not much chance he could help you – a chronic invalid for years, and it's affected his memory a bit. But I know where he has some old papers and I'll look around there and see if I can find anything. Give me your phone number or a card. Who knows, we may be able to do some business as well some time.'

When we came out through the green curtain the clergyman gave a rather timid smile. I noticed that the doll was now fully clothed and put to one side and he was examining a large silver coin.

'Yes, leave it to me,' Tennant said unconvincingly, shivering slightly, 'something will click, you'll see.'

I also felt the chill of the depressing bedroom. It seemed much less cold when I got out of the shop into the dark court.

11

AFTER THE depressing interview with the Tennants I was glad that I had an invitation for dinner and would not have to return directly to my own cold flat. Once more I realized how ill-fitted I was to be a bachelor, lacking the independence so essential to anyone who lives alone.

I was going to have dinner with my friends the Meyers, and any evening spent with them was like an oasis to me, particularly in the winter. Ben Meyer, the owner of 'The Best Chess Shop in London', had stumbled up the stairs to my office a few years previously in the hope of finding some out-of-the-way books on chess. He had obviously been disappointed in my stock of first editions and fine printing ('Picture books and fancy books – the best edition is the revised edition,' he told me bluntly later on), but had stayed to talk and we had got on well together. Indeed, I spent too much time calling in at his shop in the Royal Opera Arcade, where we would often play chess upstairs in a small room with a large window looking down on the rather romantic lamp-lit passage, so redolent of Edwardian atmosphere.

The Meyers lived in Earl's Court in a large flat that was very different from mine in its comfort and home-like appearance. It was not smart as the furniture was well used and the children left a trail of toys behind them, but it was bright with a lot of white paint and gay wallpapers, and usually resounding with good music or conversation.

Ben was easy to get on with, completely natural, frank and outspoken. Before 1937 he had been a dentist in Stuttgart, but on coming as a refugee to this country he had been unable to practise and had made a business out of his passion for chess. His uncompromising forthrightness sometimes made me a little uncomfortable, but I usually managed to dissemble this and I found his ideas stimulating. He had read very widely in English, French and German: his head was full of theories on psychology and I was often exposed to a lecture from the latest book: at other times I was hunched in nearly silent, stubborn opposition to his philosophy which was compounded of a Walt Whitmanesque love of humanity, Socialism and a simple, earthy optimism, a kind of Brechtian spirit.

Rose Meyer was a very comfortable, pleasant person to be with: she did not talk much, and when she did it was mainly about her children, but she was kind, sensitive, and communicated happiness. 'Rose is a hopeful one,' Ben had said, and I knew what he meant.

When I came out of the tube station at Earl's Court I looked up into a sky bright with stars. As I did so I was shut off for a moment from the blocks of flats around me and in touch for once with something much more real than the city's streets. Some indistinguishable scent in the night air suddenly reminded me of a similarly clear, frosty night in 1939 when I had been skating with my younger brother.

We had gone with two girls to Ruislip reservoir during one of those periods, rare in England, of thick snow and hard ice. We had got there at about ten o'clock and found it deserted, approaching the water through a wood, stumbling in little drifts of snow and then crunching on stiff leaves. We had put on our skates while sitting on humps of frosted grass by the reedy edge and then sailed out, shouting wildly, careering in enormous circles over the dark lake. There were patches of ripples in the ice and it had cracked and groaned ominously from time to time.

Whirling round then I had looked up once or twice at the sky and had experienced a wonderful sense of freedom as if I was skating through the night itself. Our faces stung in the wind and we raced faster and faster. After a while we felt and acted quite drunk with the speed and cold, waving our arms, calling out anything that came into our heads, laughing and grimacing. I remembered speeding down to one end of the reservoir, leaving

55

the others some hundred yards away: there I had bent down to tie a lace that had come loose, and had noticed bits of white weed imprisoned in the ice, and I spent a moment staring down into mysterious depths, veined with broken reeds. I had felt the strange inhuman atmosphere of night while I knelt with my hand tracing the frosted surface, and when I stood up for a moment I was detached and remote. As I raced back to the three tiny figures it was like re-entering the world.

12

I WAS ON the steps of the Meyers' flat, whistling loudly. This was a bad habit of mine which I had been unable to break: I had found myself whistling while waiting to see ducal libraries; I had whistled like an errand boy going along a corridor at Claridge's to meet one of my wealthiest customers. When I got to the front door of the Meyers' flat I could hear jazz faintly behind it. Ben opened the door, gave me an odd look as if he were silently suffering, and took my coat.

As we moved down the hall he called out to one of the doors, from behind which there came the sound of water running and children's voices and someone splashing in a bath: 'You hear what he's whistling now?'

Rose shouted, 'Who – Bob? So?'

Ben ignored this but shook his head and muttered as we went into the lounge, 'So it's typical and indicative.'

'Why, what's wrong with it?' I asked. 'It clashes with your Art Tatum, but is that a crime?'

'"Deep Purple" – 1938 or 1939– whenever you whistle it's that period. And if you sing, in a curiously dated imitation of the early Crosby I might add, it's the same period. In the five years I've known you ...'

'Four years,' I corrected.

'Five years,' he continued equably, 'it's the same always, and a musician of catholic taste like my own, which encompasses even swing, cannot but notice such details. "Deep Purple" – lawn tennis dances before the débâcle – long summer evenings with shadows creeping across the lawn. Such *nostalgie*! Looking back always – very bad for you. "What's past is prologue," as Shakespeare says.'

'Well, "Tiger Rag" played by Art Tatum isn't new. And you won't say there are any song writers like Gershwin or Hart today.'

'Agreed,' he said, 'but with you it's not just a preference for good songs. Forward, boy, forward! Remember what Sean O'Casey said when he was asked what was the meaning of life. "Life is to be lived" – it's as simple as that – get out and live it to the full. Don't spend it thinking about what might have been. What are you drinking – Campari?'

'Perfect.' I was used to Ben's irritating manner of putting me right, and I had to admit that his most casual comments which concerned me were often salutary, the kind of thing which returned for me to brood on during insomniac nights. He was the most relaxed person I knew. His brown face shone with health, his eyes were as clear as a child's: his black curly hair had retreated a little, evenly from his forehead, but on him it looked good, only stressing the width between his eyes. His clothes were as casual as his manner, but his brogues were polished to the colour of a freshly opened chestnut, his check trousers were newly pressed, the cream sports shirt and dark blue cardigan looked as if they had just come out of boxes. I often felt impelled to stick a pin in his way of life in self-defence, but it was hopeless. He was absorbed in his family, his business and the world in general. He was optimistic and happy. I was not.

I looked at the low wall bookcases packed with paperbacks and the complicated hi-fi apparatus that took up most of one wall. There was a large, home-made cabinet, which contained records of every kind from Mozart to Brubeck. When Ben reappeared with our drinks he put on Milhaud's 'Creation of the World' and we listened without conversation till it had finished.

Afterwards I told him about Stone's death, and my macabre experience in seeing someone so like him in the Rolls near Westminster. He was very interested in this and unusually quiet, making no comment at the end. On an impulse I went on to tell him something about the Lupin letters and the cable from Orville.

'God, you are more trusting than I thought,' he commented, 'placing confidence in an offer like that. You told me some months ago what an eccentric character he is – and now you take a cable like that seriously. He may just have sent it to impress some friends. Besides, you wouldn't want the letters in stock. I never buy anything that I don't want in my shop. Funny about how undependable people are. I had an experience the other day. An old lady toddled in to show me some lovely pieces – Cantonese – with kings about eleven inches high, all mounted on carved balls of ivory. Made her a fine offer. Two days later I saw them in a New Bond Street window, and the marked price was only just over what I had offered her. She probably sold it there because she was impressed by the set-up. You can't bank on people in business.'

'Well, there's a mystery about the letters too,' I said. 'Stone would never talk about them though I tackled him once or twice. And that was particularly odd because he obviously couldn't deny having had them as they were listed in his catalogue. I feel that they may have been involved in some curious incident in his past.'

Ben had picked up a ball-point pen in his left hand and fiddled with it, clicking the point in and out methodically. I could see he was thinking hard. 'That could be dangerous too – digging around in someone's past. Most people have got a buried problem, trouble hidden somewhere.' He gave me a hard searching look.

I wore my unmoved mask but felt very uneasy, as if a dentist were probing a bad tooth. I said nothing.

He got up. 'For instance, I've often wondered about you. A young healthy guy like you should be on top of things. I wonder why you are not. But Rose says I'm nosey and I badger you too much as it is. She's got some unhappiness too, stored in the past, like many of our race. Take her tip – don't probe around. Leave Stone's secrets – whatever they may be – alone. Come on: the lockshan soup, the potato lutkas, are calling!'

13

'SELDON SPEAKING.' I tried to keep an impatient tone out of my voice but I was irritated at holding the phone when no one spoke. It had started to ring as I entered my office door and was scooping up letters. I had got in early as usual on Tuesday mornings because the mail was often good that day, for some odd reason, with many bulky envelopes from America. I moved some of them round idly as I cradled the receiver between my cheek and shoulder, trying to guess which might contain cheques.

'Oh, is that Mr Seldon the book dealer?' The voice was that of a youngish man, rather nervous I guessed. The accent was very strong and definitely German. 'Will you kindly hold on – there is someone here who wishes to speak to you.'

There was a hint of pomposity in this and I did not reply but just waited. Suddenly I had to jerk the receiver away from my ear because of loud noises in it – my caller's instrument had apparently been dropped and banged against a wall while dogs barked into it. Then a feminine voice came on, in a fussy nasal tone. 'Sorry to bother you so early. Rather impulsive of us to phone perhaps, but it just occurred to me ... I saw a friend of yours, Mr Hayter, who acts for me, yesterday. We were chatting of this and that and I mentioned *inter alia,* that I have some books by Frederick Lupin here.'

I wondered what kind of work Hayter could be doing for her.

'Did Hayter say my interest would be in buying them?' I asked. 'I've seen most of his books, but if they were for sale ...'

'Yes, of course, I realize that. Well, they might be sold – if the price offered was a tempting one. Two of them must be valuable as they were inscribed to my late husband, you've probably heard of him, Charles St Clair. The poet.'

I made a non-committal noise and asked when I could see the books.

'More or less any time. In fact you could come along later this morning. Just give us time to tidy up a wee bit. Do you know Theobalds Road? Near Swiss Cottage Station. No 17. Actually there's no number but you can't miss it. A large green gate practically off its hinges – I must get it repaired. The house got rather run down during the war ...'

I broke in to assure her I could get there about eleven. Her voice was rather wearing after a time and there was still a chorus of yapping dogs. It seemed very peaceful in my office when the phone went back on its stand. I concentrated on my letters and, guessing right, opened three from American Libraries containing bank drafts. The next one I opened was from Margaret. Written in a large round regular hand on blue paper, faintly scented. This tiny detail just underlined her position for me. She was simply a very feminine person who had had the bad luck to get married to someone who just was not interested in all she could have given him. A newspaper cutting fluttered out when I unfolded her letter. It was an account of Stone's death.

CRAWLED FOR HELP
Collapsed in doorway

A coroner's court found that Edward Stone, of Ridley-road, Sandbourne died from injuries received when he was run down by a motor-cyclist in Sedge-lane, Christchurch. Mr Stone sustained a number of fractures including one to his skull but managed to crawl towards some cottages before collapsing. Mr John Taplow, of 7 Sedge-lane, heard the crash and ran out into the road but the motor-cyclist had not stopped and he did not at first see Mr Stone who was found by the door of No. 5. The police are trying to find the motor-cyclist involved ...

Margaret's letter also referred to the accident: 'I've had the police here, a quite pleasant man who said "there are certain puzzling features" about Edward being in the lane. Apparently it does not lead anywhere, just down to some estuary fields which are often flooded. And "according to the witness", presumably Mr Taplow, the motor-cycle came up the lane from the direction of the fields and then roared away. The sergeant wanted to know if Edward knew anyone there or had gone for some particular purpose. I suppose it seemed an odd place to visit on a miserable overcast day. But I explained his liking for remote spots and solitude, and that bad weather did not worry him. The more I think about it though the whole business is mysterious, because at first I thought it must have been some speed-crazy youth, but it seems that the people living in the cottages do not know anyone with a machine, and why should anyone speed up a lane like that? I've had a number of callers including some people in the street I've never even spoken to. Very kind of them but it does not help the terrible loneliness. When are you coming down here again? ...'

14

I REACHED Swiss Cottage station more quickly than I had anticipated and killed a little time in the arcade there as I wanted to get off on the right foot with Mrs St Clair. I often tried to visualize people from whom I was going to buy books, and to have a guess at their characteristics from letters or phone calls from them: I had Mrs St Clair tentatively sketched in as a rather tough nut to deal with – a Bohemian figure who would be careless about everything until money matters were raised.

Then I caught sight of myself brooding in a shop window, a typical worried look on my face ('From your unhappiness,' an Army psychologist had told me, 'you have made another personality, a mask which hides your true one, to deal with a world which seems harsh and cruel to you'). My square, over-wide shoulders gave my mac the look of a uniform (Sadist from the secret police, I thought) which clashed with the capacious bag I used for carrying books. For a moment I was able to study myself in a detached way. I saw a rather seedy literary pawnbroker, mechanically doing a job which no longer interested him very much, jogging through a life he found basically meaningless. There was not much bounce in my steps as I descended from the arcade.

Theobalds Road had been badly hit during the war and there was still a number of gaps in the row of tall Victorian villas. In one bomb-site, overgrown with weeds and tangled bushes, I noticed a small faded placard with the lettering 'A.R.P.' and an arrow pointing to a space where a house had stood. No 17 was more in need of paint than the others. It was very run down: in fact only some dingy curtains gave a hint that it might not be derelict. The iron gate had fallen down and was tied on with rope. There were two bells on the door: a Dr Schlintz's card was opposite one, so I rang the other.

After a minute or so there was an uproar as dog after dog began to bark. Then I could hear someone shouting at them and the dogs began to race into the hall, throwing themselves at the door, racing up and down, clawing in a frenzy.

'Boys, behave! Down! Good boys!' It was an angry voice and the door was opened by a tall, severe-looking woman. Her rather grey cheeks were brightened by symmetrical round patches of rouge on each side: her thin, pale hair was looped forward in a youthful style, partly covering her high forehead. She nodded, held out a limp hand, and kicked viciously backwards at some of the retreating, scuffling dogs. There was a squeal. 'Back boys! Mr Seldon? You must take us as you find us, I'm afraid. We are in rather a muddly jumble just at the minute.'

I murmured something in a polite tone as the door closed behind me, but mainly I concentrated on where I was going. It was very dark in the hall and the floor was cluttered with cardboard cartons and wooden boxes. There was an overpowering smell of dogs. She ushered me through another door.

'We used to own the whole of the house, of course. The Welfare State put paid to that! Now we are' – she turned and gave an unhappy grin – 'as poor as church mice.' She had a curious denture, of a kind I had not previously encountered, on which the separate teeth were insufficiently defined.

She hurried over to stop a gramophone which had finished playing and was grinding away at the end of the grooves. The room was a large one but crowded with dusty furniture: an ugly, black, upright piano was surrounded by tottering piles of newspapers; whole armies of toy soldiers were set out in methodical formations on a vast Buhl sideboard, which also held a large old-fashioned cruet and two bottles of gin. Long curtains nearly covered the window at the back of the house, but I could just see out.

'Rather jungly, isn't it? We had to let the gardener go,' she explained. 'Do sit down.'

The couch she pointed to was covered with a dusty dark green evil-smelling rug. 'Oh, here's Rudi! Mr Seldon – Rudolph Bergl, conductor of the Finchley Grove Orchestra.'

Mr Bergl, a short young man, had appeared mysteriously without a sound. She bent down quickly and lit a fat Turkish cigarette which she stuck on a gold pin. 'By the way' – she turned to me as she slumped down on a dusty pink pouffe, carelessly displaying her thin, bare, cold-looking legs – 'have you ever *read* any of those awful Lupin books? I know there is a cult for them nowadays, but actually they are tedious beyond words. But perhaps dealers don't read ...'

'In parts they are rather heavy going, but I like other bits very much,' I replied, displaying a Buster Keaton blankness.

'Yes, it's smart to like Lupin now,' she murmured mainly to herself. Then she wheeled round to face Bergl. 'To read Lupin, *c'est un nouveau frisson*, my dear.' She put out her hand and flapped it limply in imitation of a pansy gesture. 'But I've noticed the people who like him best are not those who actually met him.' She gave me a rather malicious look.

'Did you ever meet him?' I asked, in deadpan fashion.

'No, but he was an acquaintance of my husband's for some years, until Charles saw through him. I may have a photograph of them somewhere. I'll try to find it – and the books.' She left the room with a flounce of her dirndl skirt.

I was trying to place Charles St Clair. A very minor Georgian poet? I looked at Bergl. He had a severe case of stubble-trouble although he could not be more than nineteen or twenty. An enormous golliwog mop of black curls exaggerated the smallness of his chin. He smiled nervously: '*May* have a photograph! She knows she had one – this place is like a museum – she has everything of his, even his baby teeth in a tin.' He spoke in a conspiratorial whisper, rather breathlessly.

I got up from the couch, to have as little contact as possible with it, but I knew I was doomed to smell of aged dogs for the rest of the day. The room did have the atmosphere of a neglected museum. I had been in one in Italy which was just as dusty and inadequately lit. The inconsequential collections of furniture, newspapers and toy soldiers had a queer fascination. Propped up against one wall I found an old-fashioned tennis racquet with a fish-tailed handle and five broken strings. I brandished it at Bergl.

He laughed: 'You see! It was used by Charles St Clair in a mighty doubles match at Oxford in about 1910.'

There was a rusty model train set piled in one dark corner of the room with the station perched precariously on a heap of lines, and a large box full of miscellaneous toys. All the time I had been in the room I had been aware of an unexplained fidgeting noise and restrained coughs, from another corner.

Bergl followed my gaze. 'That's an aged parrot – fantastic old thing – called Romeo,' he explained. 'For God's sake don't notice it or she will get it out. Then I have to spend hours trying to catch it again and it nips – viciously!' He looked on edge.

By the filthy cruet stand on the sideboard I noticed a Ouija board and what looked like a fish-bowl: on closer inspection I saw that it was a 'witch bowl' with glass fishes suspended from floating glass bubbles in stagnant water, green and opaque.

Mrs St Clair swept in, triumphantly clutching a card box file and a tray with three cups. 'Du café, monsieur?' she said to me in a jocular tone. The coffee was very milky and obviously quite cold. When I stirred mine a segment of tough-looking skin swam up from the bottom like a sea monster and then sank slowly back.

Mrs St Clair, smelling rather musky, leant across me and displayed a large photograph. 'Lupin's not in that one but it might be of interest. It shows the Beast himself – Aleister Crowley.'

It was a photograph of a large group of people, apparently taken at a party or a night club in the twenties, with most of the ogling men in sailor costume, one wearing a cap lettered H.M.S. *Bluebird*. A young man with mad-looking eyes and a white, large-brimmed hat stared rather pathetically from a couch, sitting beside the fat, bald and assured Crowley. Before I had had a good look Mrs St Clair snatched it away.

'No, it's not really a good one of Charles. Ah, here he is with the fabulous Mr Lupin.'

The second photograph was a small sepia snapshot, inscribed in faded violet ink, 'Magdalen'. It showed the bridge as a rather shadowy background to a youth in a blazer standing in the river-garden, staring at the photographer. He had a handsome but rather weak face with big eyes; his head was surrounded by a dandelion puff-ball of thin fluffy hair which would not have lasted long. Behind him in a rather sinister pose was Lupin, half-hidden and turning away so that the scar on his cheek would not show. I noticed there were traces of stamp paper round Lupin's head as if it had been covered over at some time. I looked up.

Bergl's face, now the parrot's noise had stopped, had become quite inscrutable. His eyes, askance, wandered round the room at the level of the picture rail, as if he was trying them out for vision.

'So you've noticed my little subterfuge,' Mrs St Clair said in a slightly guilty voice. 'Confess I must and will. Truth to tell I could not bear anything I heard about Lupin. I found the very idea of him repulsive – like a cat.'

'But you have kept his books,' I said.

'I have preserved the books he gave to Charles – quite a different matter,' she countered. She produced them as she spoke. They were Lupin's last two novels, both inscribed in the same way: 'Charles St Clair, the author's friend.'

I had not previously seen any books inscribed by Lupin and knew that presentation copies from him were rare. I thought of a fair price to give her and then deducted something because of her snide remarks about dealers. 'I would offer twenty-five pounds for them.'

'Do you know, I think I might get a better price than that elsewhere,' she said quickly, and then before I could reply: 'But it is not in my nature to haggle. I am not fitted for the market-place. The deal is done. Pouch them before I change my mind. Now we'll have a little drink.'

She went over to the sideboard, running her fingers round the back of Bergl's neck as she passed. The idea of drinking gin at that time in the morning did not appeal to me but it was better than the curious coffee which I had left untouched. Mrs St Clair began to hum and move about in a restless way as if she was excited at the prospect of money changing hands. She had surprising vitality and gaiety – I could imagine her bursting out with a defiant superior chuckle on the way to the poorhouse – which I found faintly attractive. Bergl grinned behind her back.

15

THE REST of the week after my teashop encounter with Hayter proved that he was indeed at work 'trying to run down leads re Lupin', as he had put it. I began to revise my estimate of his connections after receiving several phone calls and notes from people he had contacted, who had books by Lupin for sale or some information to pass on.

But the most interesting phone conversation was a chaotic one with Selwyn Tennant, which began with odd squeaks and tee-hees about the mysteriousness of his identity.

'You won't know me, laddy. I mean the voice will puzzle you. Well, I'm practically a stranger to you – only met once, dear boy. Just this week ...'

In fact I had immediately recognized that high-pitched voice with its aggrieved whining tone.

'Not so,' I said; 'isn't it Mr Tennant?'

He was rather disappointed. 'Well, yes, it is. Fact is, I have news for you. Not from brother Stephen – no joy there, his memory for trivia quite gone, alas! But I have been searching. Found his receipt book for that funny old blitz period. And there it was, among a lot of bad debts – a copy of a receipted bill to Mr Terence Hearsay. Dated August 1943. No address unfortunately! "To printing a prospectus and setting a title-page and preliminary matter of projected book of Lupin letters, with proofs of same on two papers, £10." Marked paid by cash, old laddy. As I said, no address of the demned elusive Mr Hearsay, but perhaps his name will be some help. Glad to oblige. Call in any time – I get the occasional book and print.'

I felt reluctant to join his police-haunted coterie, but I was grateful for the name. I had already found that the address on the prospectus had long since been demolished to make room for a large block of offices, but with a definite name to follow up the search seemed much more hopeful. I had missed fragments of Tennant's message as he was apparently in the habit of turning away from the receiver from time to time as he talked, but I had the name HEARSAY written down in large caps on my blotter.

Hours later, when I was half-heartedly checking through some long-outstanding accounts, with the growing feeling of irritation and suspicion that chore always engendered, the name began to mean something vaguely in my memory. It was like trying to dredge a heavy weight out of a pond. June must have been puzzled to see me standing still, poised as I struggled to remember – I felt that even a movement might break the tenuous connection. Then the weight stopped slipping back and came out cleanly. I simply knew that *Poems by Terence Hearsay* was the title first suggested by A. E. Housman for his book *A Shropshire Lad*.

'No joy there,' as Selwyn Tennant would have said. All I knew about the shadowy figure behind the printing was that he was a literary joker who shunned identification, and that he had called off the publishing project a month or so after it had been announced.

In the Friday morning post I received another letter about Lupin, but this one was not due to Hayter's activities. It was written in that attractive but anonymous italic hand so popular with art students, on cream laid paper simply and imposingly headed 'Splay Court, Dorset'.

Dear Sir, I was recently discussing with a friend various authors whom we thought deserved to be better known, such as M. P. Shiel, Marmaduke Pickthall, Edgar Saltus and Ambrose Bierce. When we got round to Frederick Lupin, my friend mentioned that she had seen an advertisement in an old number of *Horizon* where you advertised your interest in purchasing any manuscripts or books by him. I think you may care to know that my father has a complete collection of his books, etc., including some unique things. Frankly, I do not think there is any chance of these ever being offered for sale: indeed I am sure that eventually they will go *en bloc* to my father's University Library, but you might be interested in seeing exactly what there is here. For instance, you cannot hope to purchase the manuscript of what I believe to be his last book, *Troubadour*, as we have it here, together with a group of letters to the publisher. I should be happy to show you the collection if you are ever in the neighbourhood. I have not been well and am likely to be confined here for the next few weeks; therefore I leave it entirely to you to make any appointment. This house is a few miles from Wareham, on a headland in Poole Harbour. Just off the A351 if you come by car.

Yours truly, Kate Saul.

I knew Sir James Saul's name well enough. I remembered we had once sent him some catalogues on the strength of his entry in *Who's Who*. I looked up this reference: 'SAUL, Sir James Henry Steyne, *cr.* 1936 ... *o.s.* of late Frank Dudley Steyne Saul; *m.* 1925 Sylvia Katherine Wilson; two *d.*' No details of education, but the impressive entries for clubs, appointments and industrial holdings took up most of a column. He *was* the gigantic Steyne Paper Co. with its dozens of subsidiary companies. His recreations were given as 'hunting, travel, collecting paintings and books'. He had three addresses: the one in Dorset, and others in Scotland and Zürich. I got his card out of our file for defunct and deleted addresses: we had sent him five catalogues. At the bottom was June's brief pencilled comment, 'Nothing.'

I did not normally make long trips to see books which would never be sold: I had heard that Saul was a millionaire several times over – it was obvious that I should not be able to buy anything from him. But this was an opportunity unlikely to occur again, and I could couple the trip with a call on Margaret. The pull of these coincidences was strong. I wrote a card to Miss Saul saying that I hoped to look in early on the following Monday afternoon.

16

GOLDMAN HAD arranged to call for me for lunch: to meet me, rather, at the bottom of my stairs. He had told me once, quite bluntly, that he would not climb my stairs unless he was convinced that he would make at least a fiver by doing so. As it was a Friday it was possible that we might go to Scott's instead of the rather interesting Kosher restaurant in Poland Street which he usually patronized: I would not know our destination until we approached Maddox Street; if we passed this then we were bound for Piccadilly Circus.

'Always walk to lunch, Robert – the best aperitif, the pleasantest exercise, the most beneficial there is,' he would admonish me, putting me in the position of being a slothful, sybaritic opponent he must overcome. In fact he was hardly ever out in the streets two minutes before he was anxiously looking round for a taxi.

This fairly amiable aggressiveness, part of a continual campaign to keep his place as top dog, was probably the main reason why I found him so wearing. He wanted me to lunch with him, and I found myself agreeing to do so, though I knew that conversation with him was conducive to *angst* and not to good digestion. He dictated where we should go, but would not reveal this: so putting me in the position of a blind man being led.

When we hesitated on the kerb of Bond Street he put a heavy hand on my arm as if to save me from an injudicious crossing: he always treated me like a foolish youth or some country hayseed. Once, when we had gone down an alley-way leading into Brewer Street, he had warned me that we might be approached by 'women'! He had some very good qualities: he was devoted to his wife and four daughters, treated his staff well, and could be generous, despite wanting every penny he could possibly make in a business deal; still I found him impossible to cope with and generally upsetting.

As we passed Brooklands Motors he noticed my eyes flickering over a bronze-coloured Jensen: 'Still got that fancy green car of yours?' He did not wait for an answer and so did himself out of the pleasure of hearing me confess that the green Mercedes had been a wild extravagance which had led to my overdraft becoming an impossible burden, and that it had been sold at a considerable loss. 'My wife remembers it,' he said; 'lime-green she called it. You turned up in it at the big sale at Guildford.'

I don't talk much, but with Goldman I often felt that I would like to change this and talk continually, battering him into silence with a non-stop barrage of words.

'I don't care for a flashy car,' he mused. I mentally ticked off some of Goldman's flashy possessions: his shop in Park Lane which had been accurately described as the most comfortable spider trap in London; the silver grey tie with the camel overcoat he was wearing; his pink villa in Hendon. He turned and looked at me earnestly, with just a hint of doubt in his sorrowful dark brown eyes. 'A flashy car I do not need. A first-class sober car, a Rover, I have. The new model each year ...'

Goldman was the one dealer who was sure to know something about Sir James Saul: I wanted to ask him what he knew, but I never seemed able to extract any information from Goldman. On the rare occasions when I had tried I had found out nothing and usually let slip something I wanted to keep to myself. One memorable, exhausting lunch-time I had had the name of my wealthiest American customer jerked out of me, as if from a hypnotist's victim. I knew that Goldman had been insistent about this lunch because he wanted to find out what was happening to Stone's books. Could I get him to swop some information?

As we walked I found myself puzzling again about Goldman's height. He seemed shorter than myself now, but at other times, particularly when he was behind his desk, he conveyed the impression that he was looking down when he talked to me. His trick of changing size was another superb weapon, like his elephant-thick skin, his absolute determination and persistence, in the war of attrition he waged against me; but, for once, I felt determined too.

When we were seated at the counter just inside the door at Scott's I felt that it might be easier than I had expected. He was smiling happily as he sat in his usual awkward way on the high stool, looking as if he might slide off at any time, his lap covered with a handful of paper napkins which kept slipping down and making a pile below his feet. He tasted the excellent thick tomato soup and then grinned amiably. He seemed to be in a benevolent mood.

'How, I am thinking, Robert, can we help poor Edward's widow? Now let me be frank. Have I pursued this subject to the point of seeming a nuisance?' His eyes were wide and guileless as he sipped his glass of Sancerre. 'Then let me explain. Now there are some books there that are just too rich for your blood – I must be frank. I doubt in fact if you have ever seen them.'

His rudeness seemed a clumsy weapon. I began to dissect my sole with care and precision as I replied, 'On the contrary, Felix, I think I was on rather better terms with Edward than you were.'

'Oh, I know you were friendly with him. But he was a hard-headed business man. There was a secret shelf of books he showed to very few people. Anyway, it's a simple thing to resolve. Have you seen the books behind the panel?'

'No. I didn't know he had any secret shelves. How very odd!'

'You see!' he crowed. 'Well, that's where the cream is – and that is the stuff that I can handle. Look, so she puts them into auction, she waits five months for the sale to come up and even then who will the buyer be? F. O. Goldman, Ltd.! So why don't we short-circuit the process? That way she saves the auction commission, I get the books now instead of next autumn, and you get a cut.'

If I could hold him to paying a fair price it did not seem a bad idea.

'All right, we'll see what we can do, on the understanding that you pay approximate auction prices. Pennington can work those out.'

'Fair enough,' he said. 'I just want to do a little business. That's not much to ask.' He chewed meditatively on some succulent smoked salmon. 'Here, have a sweetener.' He eased a slim packet of five pound notes from his wallet.

'No thanks, Felix. It would not buy you anything. Mrs Stone said she will want my advice and I shall see what I can do about you being called in. But – well, you know how unpredictable women are.'

'That's true.' He frowned and sighed.

'Now, if that is settled, will you do me a favour?' I asked. 'You know most of the big collectors. Have you had any dealings with Sir James Saul?'

His reply zipped out: 'He wouldn't buy those books. He isn't interested in colour plates and that is all there is in the cache.'

'No, this has nothing to do with Stone. I'm just curious about Saul. Have you ever sold him anything?'

'Sure I have.' Goldman tried to look modest but his voice went down an octave. 'You know some people have called me the Duveen of the book world.' He shrugged. 'I'm the last one to say it's true, but you don't get that kind of reputation without tangling with the big boys. As you ask, I can give you some very good advice about Saul. In one word – don't! And it's all the same whatever the deal is. Forget it.'

He carefully selected a toothpick from a little bundle as if he was choosing a golf club and got to work on something intransigent that was worrying him, behind the screen of his left hand in the continental fashion that I found more off-putting than an open attack. I concentrated on my coffee until he had finished the operation.

'Look, kid.' I knew that some kind of favour was coming my way as soon as I heard this. 'Saul's an impossible kind of a man. Keep away from him. You'll end up in a complicated deal which you can't handle.' He looked round to see if anyone could overhear him. 'You know I don't gossip.' It was true that small talk which did not lead to business did not interest him much and I nodded. 'Well, I once heard an unpleasant rumour about him. Just a story, mark you. Nothing positive. It was when I was buying some books in Amsterdam last year. I heard a tale from a dealer there who knows everything that goes on. He said that Saul had come close to being charged by the police with an assault. Sounds funny when you consider that Saul is more or less an invalid, with a dicky heart, but it was said that he had some kind of bodyguard, a great tough whom he sent out into the street in the Blue Lamp area, to pick fights with anyone who came along. Saul was supposed to have had a room there and sat by the window, in an invalid chair, in the dark, just watching. Anyway, this tough beat up a sailor so badly that he nearly passed out, then the police came along and caught the bruiser in the room with Saul. They couldn't prove that he was implicated, but they had their suspicions. What kind of man does that for kicks? Here, do you want to see a photograph of him?'

I was surprised by this question, but he was already tugging out the big pigskin wallet again and extracting a folded paper.

'You see, that's the Big Room at Christie's. The sale of a 23.7 carat step-cut diamond for a world record price. I kept it because it shows Sarah, there next to me, sitting at the table.'

I looked at the cutting and saw Goldman and his wife at the baize-covered table.

'Now that's Saul. He did not make a bid, though he could have bought the ring a hundred times over. I don't know why he was there.'

Goldman pointed at a thin, tall man with fair or grey hair and a small clipped moustache standing underneath a large tapestry to the left of the auctioneer's desk. Some women were looking at the photographer, one in particular straining forward so that her face should show. Saul, however, was looking down at his bowler hat.

'Yes, that's Sir James. Before he had his stroke, of course. A very nasty specimen. But what a brain! He makes mincemeat of people. Well – most people.'

Goldman did not expand this, but I understood that he meant that I would end up as mincemeat where he had escaped. I had one more look at Saul's enigmatic face. There was just a slight trace of a smile. It might have been Goldman's formidable warnings but the expression did seem unusual – that of a person completely self-contained, aloof, impervious. I wondered what his daughter would be like.

75

17

I SLEPT BADLY and got up before six on the morning I was going to Splay. There was a strong wind howling down the dark frosty street outside my window, yet I had a feeling it was going to be a fine day. Then the weather forecast confirmed that it would be mainly dry and sunny in the south-west with strong variable winds. In the bath I could hear the wind coming up the pipe: a sad haunting sound prophesying extinction and nothingness, it seemed to me. 'You indulge yourself with melancholy as a matron does with chocolates,' Ben Meyer had said to me. And it was true.

I took a bottle of Guinness and a mug from my tiny larder. After a quick visit to see the mail at my office, I bought some ham and cheese sandwiches at Jolly's: and with these in my brief-case I was all set for a winter picnic lunch, so that I could arrive at Splay just after two.

By the time I had got to Waterloo the pattern of the weather for the day was set with a pale blue sky marked with only a few high clouds. The station was full of people trotting along to the cheerful piped-in music. I found an empty carriage and had a look at my map. Splay Point looked out across the Wych Channel to Brownsea Island which I knew was a bird sanctuary, and then to the open sea in Poole Bay. I straightened my tie in the dark mirror.

I was off on a jaunt, a kind of holiday, but the nervous face in the glass might have been that of someone who had just been arrested. 'A hideous mask upon my mind, which not only disfigures but nearly suffocates it,' George Darley had written about his stammer. I was habitually dogged by a tense feeling of depression; it was no wonder that positive people like Meyer found me irritating.

There was a photograph in the carriage, alongside the mirror, of an old-fashioned seaside scene, the promenade at Shanklin. There were men in long-legged, rather obscenely clinging bathing costumes, donkeys which would be dust by now, and children who would be middle-aged. A large group of people was gathered admiringly round an ambitious sand-castle, and, just putting out to sea, three boys in a rowing boat.

I stood staring at these events which had taken place perhaps some thirty years before, peering at and identifying various objects on the beach, until I felt that I was in the grip of an odd malaise. It was just like unlocking a door into the past, one I had kept closed for years. With a confusion of half-remembered scents and places, a series of scenes came into my mind. I remembered plainly standing on the railway platform at Southampton on the way to the Isle of Wight in the late 1920's. My brother had asked to be held up in front of a scent machine which gave out a puff of violets (the same odour which had lingered on Margaret's letter) in exchange for a penny. I remembered one glorious baking hot afternoon when we had gone out sailing with two boys who had their own boat, and the adventure of being marooned for an hour or so.

Then, against my will, the memory led me on to Italy. Naples in July 1944. The Via Roma in glaring sunlight, crowded with G.I.s and hideous whores queueing outside the U.S. Prophylactic Stations: one nightmarish old tart daubed with ludicrous make-up and drenched in perfume. The streets stinking, covered with rubbish and clouds of flies. Our small Signals unit had just returned from Trasimene and we were at a loose end until our c.o. returned. Rumour had placed him in the centre of the Partisan country north of Camerino where the PPA was supposed to operate. On 12th July 1944 I was free from twelve o'clock, and I had wandered round the city noting some of the boastful Fascist slogans, still ironically in evidence on posters and white-washed walls. In the Piazza Dante, painted on a wall, I remembered, 'VV IL 1924! VV IL 1922! DUCE! VINCERE! CREDERE, OBBEDIRE, COMBATTERE.'

Then I had returned for a meal at our billet and little Smithson had told me to report at once to the c.o. The H.Q. was in a side street running up from the promenade and a closed-up fish restaurant on a pier. I could see it quite plainly in my memory, and a torn cinema poster, and hear a drunk American truck-driver singing, 'Shadows intertwining in the yellow light. Gave away our secret ... We meet again, Marlene ...'

When I had knocked I heard Major Klingel saying to Captain Johnston (the banal words engraved somewhere deep down in my mind), 'A regular balls-up! What a shower!' 'Who was on the flank?' 'Oh, all kinds of odds and sods. The Nicolo band somewhere, and Popski's lot round Tolentino ...'

I had knocked louder and they had heard the second time. When I entered Johnston looked up, rather annoyed, as if I was spoiling something. Klingel appeared pale, more ill at ease than I had seen him before. I had been searching my mind for any possible Army 'crime' but now I knew it was something more serious. His expression had produced the typical coward's reaction on my part, the tensing up of the body, the stomach turning to water. And the coward's attempt to alleviate the blow by foreseeing it. But I had not succeeded that time.

'Sit down, Sergeant,' he had said, gesturing at a stool by his desk. 'There is just no good way to break very bad news ...' I could see a small nervous tic in his cheek. 'A terrible blow for you, I'm afraid. We've heard from the police through Army H.Q. that your family's house ... destroyed by one of these new weapons ... a flying bomb.'

I could hardly take in his words. My coward's imagination had let me down for once and finally, for ever since that day all other bad news was judged to be relatively unimportant and had a dull foresuffered quality about it.

'Not quite definite about casualties – the message, I mean,' interjected Johnston.

'I don't think that Sgt Seldon would want to be given any false hopes. No, the position,' Klingel added, standing up and walking to the window, 'is that this fiendish plane or bomb hit the house at about one o'clock on Saturday – it was a total wreck and the neighbours believe that the whole family was there at lunch. I'm terribly sorry, Seldon. But, due to various complications, as Captain

Johnston said, we are not absolutely sure what the picture is. Fortunately we are going back to Bari, so I can arrange immediate compassionate leave, and we've laid it on for you to go home by Dakota.'

And home I had gone to be shown, by two solicitous wardens and a police constable, tidy piles of bricks. My worst childhood dream had come true. Our old piano was jammed in one wall looking out at the street with its top ripped off and the keys gleaming in the sun like a giant's mouth of broken teeth. On a splintered chair I had found one of my brother's school magazines. Probably in the explosion it had been blown high in the air and then by a freak chance had fallen back intact. The house next door had been hit and partly destroyed but the farther wall was still standing with a washbasin held to it by a pipe, like a surrealist painting. And half a flight of brickdust-covered stairs leading nowhere. By chance the things in our larder were little damaged and had been carefully gathered together in a large wicker basket.

'Nothing gone from there, Sergeant,' said one of the wardens, with pride in the probity of our suburb and quite unaware of the irony of his statement.

There was a bustle as a woman with three small children, a folding pram and a kitten got into the carriage. I helped her and then stared down at my map. For years I had been afraid to face this memory: it had been like a wound a patient dares not uncover. I had tried to cover it deep with a deadness, a numbing of feeling and a cynicism about all things. Had I come to the point where I could hope to do better than that?

18

A BUS GOING to Corfe Castle dropped me on a side road leading across heathland to Splay. Soon I found a brick wall which I knew surrounded the Court. 'Four miles of bricks, sir,' the conductor had told me. 'Next longest wall to Lulworth Castle's, in this area.'

I sat on a gate in a fence facing the wall and ate my lunch. The sky was completely blue and clear; there was not much warmth in the sun, otherwise it might have been a fine spring day.

I admired the smooth clipped green of the bank which sloped up to the fine old bricks. As I crossed into the road I heard a car: a racing change down and then hard braking. I turned to see a dark green Jaguar XK 140 pulling up behind me. The car came level with me and the driver leaned across to open the door on my side. He wore a dark grey suit, white shirt with buttoned-down collar and black knitted tie. His hair was thinning from a pronounced widow's peak but there were a lot of coarse hairs on the backs of his hands and a few odd ones appeared over the top of his tie. He took sun glasses from his tired, sad grey eyes. He needed a shave.

'Going to the house?' he asked in a rather hoarse voice with a faint German accent. His mouth turned down at the corners and he had a sharply dissatisfied expression. 'There is only the Court up this road,' he explained. 'My name's Berning. I work there. You're not expecting to see Sir James? He's abroad.'

'No – Miss Saul – about some books.'

'Oh, I see.' He put his glasses back and regarded me for a moment in silence. I noticed a badly mended scar at the side of his neck. I had the impression that I was being weighed and dismissed. He slammed the door without offering me a lift and the car sped off with a stab of the accelerator and a good deal of rear wheel spin.

I felt reasonably certain that I would not last long in a fight with Mr Berning; he managed to convey an impression of unusual strength, he gripped the steering wheel as if he might throttle it; but I knew that I could drive a fast car better than he did.

The Court entrance gates of eighteenth-century ironwork, flanked by massive stone piers each carrying a gryphon's head, opened on to a wide white gravel drive. The copse which lay behind the walls soon petered out into spurs of rhododendrons and then I could see the house standing on high ground about a quarter of a mile away in parkland dotted with giant beeches and deodar cedars. It was a Queen Anne stone house, framed by crescents of great lime trees. About a hundred feet from it two cars were parked by some old stables, hidden from the house by a clump of box trees. One was a new, small Morris but I could not resist having a quick look at a Rolls Continental Phantom II, the model which Ivan Everden created for Sir Henry Royce in 1930. Painted saxe-blue with herring scales blown over it and finished off with coats of lacquer to give an iridescent oyster finish. I peered into the stables to see if a Bugatti Royale was lurking there, but it was empty.

Beyond the stables the drive ran up a gradual slope and was barred by a wide white gate with large posts and urn-topped finials, presumably to stop cars driving up to the house. This had been swung back and Berning's Jaguar had gone through and swirled round in the gravel just in front of the shallow steps which led to a stone balcony. I looked up for a moment before I went to ring the bell; there was a balustraded attic story over the main cornice, and a cartouche with a shield supported by gryphons over the front door, the motto so worn as to be illegible.

A well-scrubbed man in an immaculate white jacket and black trousers opened the door and guided me through a surprisingly bright hall with tables bearing great vases of white and gold chrysanthemums.

'I believe we'll find Miss Saul in what we call the "office", sir. I know she has just come in from riding, and I think she went in there.'

He knocked on a door and entered. I followed close on his heels but regretted doing so once in the room as it was obvious we were disturbing the occupants. Berning, with his tie loosened and collar button undone disclosing the top of a very hairy chest, was seated behind a desk lolling back on two legs of a chair, holding himself suspended by his feet on a ledge. He was cradling a phone and smoking a brown cigarette, squinting through smoke at the ceiling.

'Yeah, Willi? Yeah, versteh.' He palmed the phone to look at us. His eyes were hard.

The girl was about twenty-five. She was dressed in black jodhpurs and a scarlet sweater, holding a black riding jacket. With her other hand she playfully pointed her crop at Berning's throat as if to topple him from his precarious position.

Berning said quietly into the phone, 'Look, Willi, I'm tied up just now. I'll get back to you. Yeah. Thanks.' His face twisted into a grimace towards me, half sneer and half recognition as he slammed the phone down.

'A Mr Seldon to see you, Miss.'

'Mr Seldon?'

'Yes,' I said. 'You wrote to me about the Lupin books in your father's library.'

'*I* wrote to *you* about *books?*' The girl sounded as if she were trying to stifle amusement and disbelief. Berning looked like a badly trained tiger waiting to pounce. I noticed that the top half of the wall on my left was of semi-opaque glass with an engraved border; in the centre there was a motto: 'THE SAME FORCE IMPELS US ALL.'

The girl continued to regard me with amusement. She was very attractive – tall and slim with high small breasts sharply outlined by the tight sweater. Blue eyes and fair, tawny hair slightly dishevelled by her ride. A sapphire ring the size of a postage stamp on her hand. I was sorry to see her nails were painted crimson. She laughed and pointed her crop at my companion.

'You've goofed again, Lawrence! It's Kate he wants to see. You know I don't read books!'

Lawrence looked grave. 'I do make mistakes, Miss.' He made it sound like a submerged joke.

She said to me, 'I'm Emma Saul – you'll probably find Kate in the white room. Will you take Mr Seldon there, Lawrence?'

The old man stumped out of the room and I followed him in silence. The white hair on the back of his neck looked like clean shavings freshly fallen from a carpenter's bench. He muttered something about being only human and Miss Emma being the one who always had the visitors and Miss Kate hardly ever seeing anyone. We walked down a long gallery running practically the length of the house with lots of windows on the left hand side and paintings on the right.

Uncluttered spaciousness was the main impression I had of Splay Court. The pieces of furniture I saw were of fine quality including an old cypress-wood chest, but they were well spread out. There was white paint in abundance and a golden coloured carpet covered the gallery floor. As we passed hurriedly along I had tantalizing glimpses of a Jean Fouquet, a Charonton and a charming Limbourg landscape.

Folding white doors at the end of the gallery opened on to a magnificent white and gold room with a stucco ceiling. Lawrence called 'Mr Seldon, Miss' to someone seated in a large chair facing french windows along the south wall, motioned me forward and turned on his heel. There was no reply from the seated girl and I approached her chair, feeling embarrassed when I saw that she was asleep.

On a table by the arm of her chair there were two books, one Erskine Childers' *The Riddle of the Sands* and the other reversed so that I could not see the title, blue-rimmed spectacles, an empty coffee cup and a silver vinaigrette.

She was the same build as her sister but with paler hair and skin. She wore a thick, navy-blue sweater with a big collar, a grey and blue tweed skirt, blue woollen stockings and highly polished, brown moccasin loungers. I judged her to be a year or two younger than her sister. I stood very close to her chair for a moment, near enough to see that her eye-brows were silvery-fine and even, and to catch a fresh coal tar soap smell. Her hands lay in her lap showing the nails clipped short, free of polish but well kept, with large white moons.

I moved past the sleeping girl to the window. I felt rather foolish for the second time in a few minutes, but it was entirely Lawrence's fault and I did not fancy finding him again. I looked at the superb *verde antico* marble fireplace. A few gilt chairs and a small china cabinet were lost in this ballroom. It gave me an odd feeling to regard this lovely sleeping girl. She had a child-like air of defenceless innocence.

19

I HEARD HER stirring behind me and turned to see that she had opened her eyes. She jumped up. I babbled away rather in my confusion: 'I'm Seldon – you wrote to me. I'm so sorry about this but your house-man Lawrence showed me in and left before he knew you were asleep, and I'd already barged in once on your sister ...'

'Oh, Lawrence,' she said. 'A slight tendency to be off-hand prevents him from being perfect. "Farouche independence" my father calls it. Well, anyway – how do you do.' She put her cool hand firmly into mine. 'So you met Emma?'

'Yes, and Mr Berning.'

'Alfons? I didn't know he was back, and one usually knows that fairly soon!' She had an easy, friendly smile.

She stood by me at the window. Outside the lawn descended in two terraces, on the left to a stone pool, a fountain and yew topiary, on the right to a tennis court Farther to the right the land rose steeply past brick walls surrounding kitchen gardens and arbours to a wooded headland and the sea.

'Do you like it here?' she asked.

'Yes, it's a wonderful house – and this view.'

'Spoilt, alas, by that tennis court,' she frowned. 'Look, let's go and see the books now, then we'll have a walk round before tea.'

We left the big room by a door which brought us to an oak staircase. 'Twin stairways – a fine conceit, I think,' she said. 'Do tell me – what do you think of Alfons?'

'Well, I only met him for a minute, but he gave me the impression of boundless energy.'

She laughed. I noticed that her eyes were a darker blue than her sister's and that her teeth were large and very white.

'Very diplomatic! Of course,' she went on, 'I should not have asked you about Alfons. But I find it rather fascinating. Everyone sees him differently. Actually he's one of my father's personal assistants. He calls himself a trouble-shooter – a horrid word! Em sees him as a kind of knight ...'

'And you?' I asked.

She hesitated, smiling. 'Ah well, my reaction is an involved one. I have a natural prejudice against people who are liable to jump on to mantelpieces. I suppose I'm an intellectual. Basically a lazy, cowardly type – exactly the opposite to Alfons. But secretly I envy him all that energy. He's a great help to my father. Especially now.'

We had passed along a dark blue carpeted passage and turned into a large room in which stood six identical walnut bookcases.

'My father has been very ill, you see. Not like me – I only had appendicitis. He had thrombosis, and it's left him very groggy and partially crippled. Alfons does most of his travelling for him now. My father is in Switzerland – he has his main office there. But there are paper and pulp mills in Canada, New York and London offices and a biggish factory in Germany. If you had been in the room more than five minutes with Alfons you would inevitably have heard him phoning for a plane reservation or looking up a time table to go somewhere ... While I do most of my living vicariously, with these.' She pointed to one of the bookcases.

I went towards the case she indicated and saw that one shelf was filled with Lupin's books. 'I'm rather surprised that you have read Lupin,' I said.

'Why – because his books are odd? But that is just the kind of thing I have read.' She grinned. 'I know the main highways of English Lit. far from well, but I've frequented some of the byways. It's the eldritch, the orchidaceous, that appeals to me. What's that poem by Hopkins about everything original, spare, strange ... Typical that I've read Hopkins, but not Bridges: Lupin, but not Gissing.'

She moved to the window. 'I would like to change this view – it would be nicer to be the other side of St Alban's Head and see that wonderful series of great white cliffs going past Lulworth towards Weymouth. Of course when we took Alfons to Lulworth he insisted on swimming through the Durdle Door, which the locals look on as a suicide bid.'

I had just come across Lupin's manuscript of *Troubadour* bound in citron morocco, with a file of letters at the end. It was a fairly typical series of complaints, threats and pleas for money. They were lively letters, but I stifled a mental yawn as I leafed through them. It was funny, but after having gone to some trouble to see these Lupin things I did not find them half as interesting as the attractive girl who stood with her back to me.

I pulled out a first edition of *A Goat's Paradise*. Immediately I opened the book I saw that a few printed pages of smaller size were loosely inserted at the front. It was Stone's Catalogue of the Lupin letters. The initials R.B.T. were written in pencil on the front wrapper. I showed this to Miss Saul. 'Is this your father's writing?'

'Oh no, that's much too studied for him. He always scrawls.'

It struck me as just remotely possible then that Saul had been behind the Petronius Press affair and I looked carefully along the remaining Lupin volumes to make sure that the morocco one of Ibiza letters was not staring at me from the shelf. But it was not there, and it seemed rather an anticlimax to examine the other things. I was unlikely ever to have the opportunity of seeing such a complete collection of Lupin again, and I was sure the books in the other five cases probably rivalled the paintings I had caught a glimpse of in the gallery, but I could not work up an interest in them. While I looked rather idly round the room, I was wondering whether I could give the initials R.B.T. any significance, and how soon I could suggest to Kate that we went for our walk.

I was pleased to hear her say, 'Look, it's clouding over a little. Shall we nip out while there is still some sun? You could always come back up here after tea if you wanted to.'

I had been thinking about Goldman's description of Sir James and found it very hard to believe in the pleasant company of his daughter.

'Would I be terribly rude if I asked you to tell me something about your father?' I asked tentatively.

'Not at all – he's an interesting person. Did you know that he built up the business from quite a small family affair?'

'No, I've noticed his name in the papers occasionally, but usually in connection with buying pictures.'

We left the house by a door in the west wall. Looking up, I could see a carving of Diana the Huntress in relief under the cornice. The sun was very low now, flushing the surrounding sky and a few dark grey-blue clouds. Walking along with Kate, looking at her profile, I could see that her top lip, provocatively curved, projected very slightly.

'My father.' She reflected. 'I hope you will understand that I am not trying to bask in reflected glory. And that this will not sound conceited. My father is an exceptional person. He has enormous vitality – just as much as Alfons, or at least he did have until this heart trouble. He sets himself difficult objectives and then achieves them. I wonder sometimes though if this makes for happiness.'

'How do you mean?'

'Well, I think he has done the things he wanted to do – but perhaps he finds his achievements a little empty. Then again – please believe that I don't usually babble on like this about him – I wonder if he really likes success.' She stopped and pointed up to the right. 'Do you see that little house?' Tucked away in some rather untidy woodland on the hilly ground I saw a small white building. 'Em and I call it his folly. It has been closed since the middle of the war. A perfectly sound building which would make a super studio. But he closed it up and apparently he will just let it become derelict. It's funny, but he has rather an obsession with ruins and deserted places. He's taken me to Lulworth Castle on three occasions, and spent hours just wandering round that burnt-out shell. Of course, the setting is superb but I think he is fascinated by the desolate atmosphere of the ruined house. "Nothing but change and decay all around me" – I'm misquoting terribly but you know what I mean. And sometimes he runs movies of the devastation from bombing in German cities ... No, he's too complicated a person to be happy just with success.'

'And your mother?' I asked.

'My mother is dead.'

'Oh, I'm sorry.'

'No need to be – it happened when I was very young. I can barely remember her.'

We passed through the cool pallid light of a shady gorge. On our right the now sharply rising land was covered with tangled undergrowth. A short stretch of dry springy grass led to a small beach. From the cliff a stream ran down between clumps of samphire. Kate led the way across the stony edge and then along to some rock pools.

The sun had sunk over the headland, and in the shadow the scene looked quite different.

'Now this appears a rather desolate place,' I said, looking at the tide's debris laid out in neat lines along the littoral. There were white, peeled sticks, a large crab's broken carapace, a gull's shrivelled skeleton and dark long strands of uprooted kelp lying parallel with the wet sand.

'Yes, it's the sun forsaking us,' she said quietly. 'It makes you feel as if you must hold your breath. This kind of atmosphere does have an eerie fascination.'

We looked out to sea. By a small island we could see a solitary yacht creeping back before the approaching darkness, and farther off a small winking light. Kate bent down by a pool and we became absorbed in its tiny private world. She dipped her hand under the still surface and moved her fingers slightly, closing the fringed anemones into dull red bulbs, and sending the nearly invisible shrimps shooting off into the weed. She scooped at something on the bottom of the pool and when she raised her hand I saw she had a tiny starfish floating in her palm: she let the water drain away and stared with a rapt expression at the coral coloured star, which looked like a baby's hand. I could remember feeling wonder like that, but had not experienced it since I was a schoolboy. Now starfishes, like the gulls crying above our heads, were just things to me.

The sea wind whistled round our ears and ruffled Kate's hair; it made grooves in the sand and tugged at the bunches of fat samphire.

Kate stood on tiptoe and pointed. 'Look, you can just see the Folly from here – like a haunted house! Fantastic the difference the light makes.'

20

For one reason and another the short trip back from Splay to Sandbourne took quite a time. Berning and Emma Saul had gone in his car to the pictures at Weymouth, and a gardener who did some chauffeuring was not immediately available. He turned up eventually in an old Austin Seven, transferred to the small Morris and took me to Wareham just in time for me to miss a train.

In the unheated waiting-room and the old-fashioned train which seemed to inch its way round Poole Harbour, I found I was thinking more and more about food. With some idiotic idea of appearing ascetic or non-hoggish, I had eaten only two bridge rolls and one tiny cake for tea at Splay. Before that I had had four sandwiches for lunch and a cup of coffee for breakfast. Now I was obsessed with the meal Margaret might have prepared. I had lunched and dined there on many occasions and always her cooking had been perfect: salade Niçoise, sole bonne femme, grilled fillet steak with tomatoes and mushrooms.

The train jogged indifferently along and then ground to a halt. At this most inappropriate time I began to hear Bernard Orville discoursing, as he had done once in my office, on why he disagreed with many of his compatriots' view of English cooking. 'Of course you must know your way about, Seldon. Most people from the States make the mistake of rushing into the first restaurant in Soho and expecting a Parisian cuisine. But here, well, when you know where to go ...' He had gone gloatingly, almost lovingly, through a catalogue of meals. 'There's boiled turbot and salmon at Sheekey's, both good; or perhaps a jumbo-sized wedge of halibut with parsley sauce, that's good too. *Scallops Waleska* at Wheeler's – very good. Sirloin of beef and flavoury saddle of mutton at Simpson's – good oh, very good, perhaps with giblet soup – excellent soup that, Seldon. The kidney-and-oyster pudding is good, too. City-wise, why there are chophouses like the Coltman's Clarence! Steaks at the George and Vulture ... curried turbot at Sweeting's ...'

With difficulty I turned off the internal broadcast of Orville's unending list by thinking about Alfons Berning. He would be, I estimated, almost my exact contemporary. I found that I had an affinity with most people of my own generation, those who had grown up between the two wars, comparatively unspoilt in childhood, knowing what a scarcity of money meant and seeing real poverty around them. I did not like the look of Berning, but I thought I could understand him.

His childhood would probably have been much more austere than mine. Quite possibly he had known what it was to be really hungry. I had seen a lot of faces like his among men of the SS Panzer Divisions – tough, uncompromising, defiant faces. I remembered talking to one, a lieutenant with the Iron Cross First Class and German Cross in Gold who had been taken prisoner at Stavelot. He had shown me in derision a battered copy of *The Führer's Orders of the Day*: 'To maintain peace ... In a just cause ... The war which has been forced upon us ... I, Adolf Hitler ... Supreme Commander of the Wehrmacht ... destined by Providence ...' He had been completely disillusioned about Nazism, though he had been drenched in it as a boy and his brother was a *Kreisleiter*, but he was altogether bitter – he had the feeling that his generation had been cheated out of any chance of happiness.

I wondered where Berning had been during the war, how and when he had got the wound in his neck. I realized that to have his job with Saul he must be a good deal more than an extrovert gymnast. He would have to be a linguist, have a first-class brain, and generally to use more tact than had been in evidence during our fragmentary meetings. In any circumstances I felt that I should disagree with Berning about most things, but we shared a common experience in having lived through the same years. Kate Saul was probably only ten or twelve years younger, but that period was an important one, giving us quite a different outlook.

21

Coming out from the station at Sandbourne I was met by an icy blast of wind: it had veered round to the southeast and was blowing in hard from over the dark sea. The handful of passengers from the train hunched their shoulders against it and dispersed into empty streets. In a ten-minute walk I passed only two people, a young laughing couple. I felt keenly jealous of them and wished again that I had met someone like Kate when I was about her age.

Walking along the cul-de-sac to Stone's house it seemed as if I might be on a deserted planet. I had not seen anyone since leaving the main part of the town and there were no lights in the houses I passed. I looked up at the brilliant, cloudless, dark blue sky glittering with stars and a half moon. I was empty, cold and depressed.

But the feeling went off as I rang the bell and the house came to life with high heels skittering along the polished floor. Margaret practically ran to the door and rattled it open.

'Oh, Bob! Do excuse me if I'm terribly windswept.'

She moved her warm hand as if to shake mine, but took hold of my wrist, so that I felt her pointed nails.

'I've been out shopping all day. Quite a spree! And since then I've been in rather a whirl. What do you think of these?' She lifted a foot. She was wearing a green silk frock with a flame-coloured cardigan and green Cuban-heeled shoes. I knew she was proud of her tiny feet.

'Fine. Did you have much difficulty finding them?'

'Fantastic! Most assistants seem to think I'm mad when I ask for size two and a half. Look, go into the bookroom. I think it's cosier in there. I'm just going to put the finishing touches to some chicken sandwiches. And I've opened a bottle of red wine – to take the room's temperature – that's right, isn't it? I don't know if it's a good one ...'

It seemed that I was doomed to continue with a cold diet but there was the wine to give some warmth. It was a rather rare one, a Château-bottled Chinon from Touraine, with an intense, pure taste. I poured two glasses and greedily began to drink mine. Deep coloured, rich in perfume and pervaded by an unmistakable taste of the Cabernet grape, even the first glass had its effect.

'It's a funny old world that we live in, De dah, di-de dah, di-de dah': Charlie Hayter's continual saying seemed particularly appropriate to this moment. My feeling of unease in this room had gone; it had been replaced by one of confidence and familiarity, as if I were a husband impatiently waiting for the little woman to produce an overdue meal. Margaret had made some small changes in the room. Edward's desk had been pushed up against the wall, and his papers and reference books tidied away. There were now two vases of flowers, some small bronze chrysanthemums standing on a table where Edward had kept a decanter, and some large, unreal-looking, waxy cream ones on the floor.

I went over to the table and picked up Stone's photograph. Looking at it closely a few details, such as the darker fuller hair, made me realize that it had been taken many years ago. I turned it round: on the back of the frame there was a gilt label, 'Mandragora Studios, 15 Garsington Street, w.c.1.' Finding the address of the 'Petronius Press' in that casual way gave me an odd sensation. It had the unreality of a discovery made in a dream, and I scribbled the name Mandragora on the back of my cheque-book with a feeling that it might well vanish before I looked at it again. The business name 'Petronius Press' had not been registered at Bush House, as required by law, but irrationally I felt that the 'Mandragora Studios' would have been.

Margaret bustled in with a large plate of chicken sandwiches decorated with a sprig of parsley. I had refilled my glass. She had removed her cardigan and the low-cut green dress set off her skin and the colour of her eyes which glinted with excitement.

'May I ask you,' she said in a mock-solemn voice, 'your candid opinion of one Mr Goldman?'

'Felix? Oh, he's not a bad chap.'

'He is, you know. He's phoned me twice about these blessed books.' She flopped back on the couch. 'He even gave me the address of his house in Hendon in case I wanted to contact him at short notice! "Woodman's Chase"! It sounds like something out of Sherlock Holmes – "'Woodman's Chase', cabby, as fast as you can!"' She ran her fingers through her hair and gestured her annoyance. 'He's a ghoul, that man. Or a vulture. He ought to have black-edged cards printed, "Widow's waited on" – that kind of thing. Anyway ...'

Margaret was going through the Chinon nearly as fast as I was but it did not hold back her tide of news. After three glasses I felt that I must concentrate hard in order to make any sense of what she was saying. I noticed how dark the lashes were that fringed her green tawny-tinted eyes, and the shadow and texture of the top of her breast which was like a white rose.

'Anyway ...' She paused again and I wondered if she was struggling to find some recherché adjective to describe Goldman or just having trouble with the significance of language as I was. 'I have news for Mr Goldman. No sale, and he can like it or lump it! I went to see our bank manager and he told me that, quite apart from his business account, Edward had fourteen thousand pounds there, on deposit. Isn't it fantastic? Apparently for years and years he had been drawing out about a hundred and twenty pounds each month from his business account for our expenses, etc., and religiously putting in a hundred on deposit. What do you make of that?'

'It certainly sounds rather queer. Could it have been some complicated tax fiddle?'

'I don't think so. I mean, if someone had paid him a large sum in cash he might have tried to hide that from the tax people, but not a hundred a month, year in, year out. Still, I'm not too worried where it came from. It's there – that's what counts. Why? Do you think I might have trouble about tax?'

'I don't know. I'm no expert. So the books won't be sold after all?'

'No, dear boy. What I need from you is a lowish valuation on them for probate – then I shall keep them as an investment. I say, you won't let Pennington put too high a figure on them, will you?'

'He's incorruptible, I'm afraid.' She did not comment on this but got up and walked out of the door. The exaggerated care with which she negotiated the table showed that the wine was affecting her too. After she had gone I completed my sentence. 'But I'm not.'

She was back in a minute, motioning me up from the couch.

'I've got a surprise for you. Listen!'

From the lounge next door I could hear a trombone moving into the first bars of 'Moonglow.'

'There, you never expected to hear that kind of music here!'

'Where did you get it?'

'I went round to Jacqueline and borrowed a pile of records. I wanted to see if you could dance.'

We moved off into a rather unambitious foxtrot. The space was limited and it was a long time since I had done any dancing. I was so conscious of the warmth of her skin through the thin silk, and her breasts moving against my chest, that I could not think about any fancy steps, and we just jogged round. The top of her head only came up to my shoulder, and looking down I could see coppery glints and some stray golden hairs among the dark red curls.

'How are you feeling!' I asked.

'Deliciously vague.'

Our ambling round the room would not have pleased a ballroom enthusiast but sensually it was very pleasant. And if it wasn't Artie Shaw playing 'Moonglow' it was someone very like him. It seemed so different from the last time we had been in this room. The feeling of guilt had disappeared. I was tempted to tease her about whether we should be interrupted by Ann again. She followed my erratic steps well, clinging closely to me. I moved my hand possessively on her back, holding her tight with a feeling of power and then tracing the taut line of her brassière strap.

She ran her fingers along my left collarbone and down the arm. I had an athlete's biceps, but laughed inwardly as I felt myself tense to make my belly flat. Her hands would not explore so far, but my desire to please was automatic. We began to kiss hungrily with open mouths.

I lowered her down slowly to the couch with my hands still on her back. At the top of her dress fastening there was a hook held by a tiny loop of thread and I could not get it undone. My fingers felt enormous and useless. She shuddered and made a deft movement at the back of her neck, and I slid her out of the thin green silk like a beautiful butterfly from a chrysalis. We were in a torment that would admit of no delay and she tugged with me at my clumsy jacket, her eyes aslant and seeming unseeing. Then as we became one androgynous figure she gasped and sobbed, her fists beating on my back in an ever-quickening tattoo.

22

In the morning I took Margaret her breakfast in bed and then went exploring in the bookroom. With Goldman's location of the secret cupboard in mind I looked carefully along the panelling below the bookcase and soon found a gap where one panel did not quite join the beading. It was easy to push back and disclose a shelf of bulky volumes, the cache of rare colour plate books which Edward had wanted to preserve from handling by most of his customers. Behind the books there was a card suit box. I moved the books to the desk to show Margaret that her investment had appreciated considerably during the night, and looked through the box.

Fitting in the bottom there was a thick ledger. One look inside was enough to show me that this was Stone's journal in which he had kept a record of the more interesting books and manuscripts which had passed through his hands, along with quotations and jottings of a miscellaneous kind. I had known of the existence of this book since a day early on in our friendship when he had told me that he had 'written up' a description of the coach drawings he had bought at our first meeting.

There was also an envelope containing photographs, press cuttings and odd scraps of paper. I spread these out on the blotter. Most of the photographs were of one young man: tall, with theatrical good looks but something rather cheap and off-putting about the fair, firmly waved hair and confident teeth-flashing grin. In flannels, lounge suit, flying costume or raffish blazer he looked as if he had just been dressed up for the chorus in a musical comedy.

On the back of two snapshots were the initials R.B.T. which I had found on the copy of Stone's Lupin Catalogue in the Saul library. Another was inscribed in Stone's hand: 'Ronnie (complete with Baron von Richtofen helmet and scarf) after a flip round the bay. Christchurch, May 1939.'

Pushing the photographs to one side I began to go through the newspaper cuttings. They all related to R.B.T.

FRAUDS OF A BOY OF 17

LORDLY DAYS IN BRIGHTON

Neatly dressed in a grey lounge suit, Ronald Blaize True, 17, who posed as a son of 'Lord Lucas', listened with composure and sometimes smiled at the recital of his misdeeds before Sir Harold Wallace, K.C., at London Sessions today. He pleaded guilty to a series of frauds. Mr S. A. Kitchin, prosecuting, explained that the youth's career would be extremely hard to beat for coolness and audacity. In April he had been to a firm of outfitters and obtained suits, evening dress and accoutrements to the value of £76. In May he had obtained goods to the value of £100. Afterwards he had put up at the Jermyn Place Hotel, Brighton as 'Captain Lucas' and left without paying his bill. 'It seems very easy,' remarked Sir Harold Wallace ...

YOUTH'S ARREST

IN STOCKBROKER'S OFFICE
Alleged Threat With Revolver
'Colonel' at 19

More about the exploits of a young man, Ronald B. True, alias Victor Lucas, who had represented himself as 'Lord Lucas' and also passed as a Colonel, was heard before Mr Cedric Castle at the Westminster Police Station yesterday. Charges of obtaining credit and large quantities of photographic material, etc., were preferred, the prosecutors being Messrs Everett Deane of William IVth Street, Strand, and Messrs Hedgington, Ltd., Piccadilly. Superintendent Harrison said: 'His replies to my questions being unsatisfactory, I told him that I was a police-officer and that he would have to accompany me to the police-station. He asked me to produce my warrant card. I did so. Then, without any warning, he suddenly sprang from his chair, waving a revolver, saying: "Hands up! The game is up!"'

There were a number of cuttings duplicating these accounts, but my eye was taken by a smaller one which had been mounted on a quarto sheet of paper and annotated in Stone's hand. He had dated it '12th January 1944'.

MAN FOUND DROWNED AT

CANFORD CLIFFS

Mystery, says Coroner

Ronald Blaize True, aged 24, of Victoria Villa, Hurley, Berks, was found drowned, it was stated at the Bournemouth inquest on Monday. The Coroner, Dr Ian B. Fletcher, described the death as a mystery. The deceased had been found fully dressed. 'It is quite impossible to tell how he had got into the sea,' he said. The man's mother, Mrs Violet True, said her son had left home the previous year and she thought he had joined the R.A.F. 'He had never talked of ending his life. He had always been very happy at home.' The Coroner recorded an Open Verdict.

RONALD BLAIZE TRUE

Underneath this Stone had written:

1919–1943
And what of the Underworld, O Charidas?
Great darkness.
And the resurrection?
A lie.
And the Lord of the Underworld?
A Fable. – We perish utterly.

23

'EVERYTHING IN nature is lyrical in its ideal essence; tragic in its fate, and comic in its existence.' This quotation from George Santayana was probably the most salutary of the many I discovered in Stone's journal. How apt it was in relation to Ronald True's comic existence and his end in the sea beneath Canford Cliffs. I had found the journal of compelling interest and brought it back with me to London, explaining to Margaret that it would be helpful in the valuation of some of the things in her collection.

This was true to a certain extent: for instance, I now knew that the fine bust of Shakespeare which stood in her hall had been fashioned by William Perry from Herne's Oak in Windsor Park, which is mentioned in *The Merry Wives of Windsor*. But much more interesting to me was the light it threw on Stone's character – his most private life was revealed by this mélange of business notes, aphorisms and pithy, sometimes malicious, comments about people he had met.

The journal followed me from bed to bath to tube station. From cryptic, scattered notes I pieced together the history of the Ibiza letters from the time Stone came across them until their eventual sale. He had bought them from 'Paulo' in 1938: "at his country place" at Flush, in Dorset: a rundown, home-made shack which eminently suits its little, futile, pop-eyed owner. Completely bald, and rather dirty. Of course he was not like this when Lupin knew him but one wonders how such letters ever got written to anyone so ineffectual & *silly*.'

Stone had apparently intended to keep the letters but had been forced to put then in the 1942 Catalogue due to his business falling off duing the war. '17th February 1943. Sold the Frederick

Lupin holographs to Ronnie True! No explanation forthcoming as to his sudden (? sinister) prosperity. Rather intriguing, as the last time I saw him he was jobless and quite despondent at being turned down flat by the R.A.F. Apparently his vision is far from perfect. But he was too vain to admit this before or to wear glasses – when I flew with him I was taking more of a risk than I knew! It is possible he bought the letters for a third party. He talked recklessly of publishing them, but I persuaded him that it would be folly to do so.'

Another note concerned with True was of a prophetic nature: 'R.B.T. undoubtedly the most charming but irresponsible person I have met. Truly infectious gaiety – like a glass of champagne. But any relationship with him is fraught with danger as he is liable to do anything on impulse regardless of the consequences. He reminds me continually of Stevenson's phrase, "A Bazaar of Smiling and Dangerous Chances".'

I put down the journal reluctantly to go to Sotheby's and make some bids for an American customer. As soon as I got to the top of the stairs I knew Goldman was there. 'No, sir,' he responded to some bidding in a doom-laden voice as if he was vetoing the last chance for peace at the United Nations. He had a habit of keeping up a continuous commentary on sales which did not make him popular. And his stage-whispered, belligerent remarks could be heard in the other galleries. I stood at the back of the room by the door. Turning, I found my neighbour was Tenby-Smith. Tall and slightly stooping, with a thin, bony face, Smith had the appearance of a dried-up scholar, but he had an off-beat malicious sense of humour. I liked him because he was never over-awed by the solemn atmosphere of the auction.

Goldman's large, black-suited back dominated the green table. He half jerked out of his seat as he made a petulant bid. 'Thirty bob!' he said derisively. This was on a book which every dealer knew would make at least two hundred pounds, and was his irritating method of demonstrating that he thought it was over-valued.

Smith turned to me, his eyes glinting behind smeared glasses. 'Why does he say that? It's not funny. It's not clever. It's hardly original.' And then, *sotto voce,* 'Twelve million pounds. Will you take my bid, sir? Or not, sir? A glass of water for Mr Tenby-Smith, sir! He is having one of his bad turns.'

Goldman got up from the table and wheeled round in our direction, lumbering carelessly past other people, wagging a finger ominously. Smith whispered, 'Do you think he heard me? No offence, sir! Only a joke, sir!' and did an elaborate faked limp further into the room toward the auctioneer's desk. But Goldman's finger and acerbity were intended for me.

'Now, Robert,' he said, standing in front of me and blocking out the sale, 'no more dragging your feet.' He nodded portentously. 'I'm banking on good news about the Stone books. What's the position?'

'Hopeless, I'm afraid. She has made up her mind not to sell. Well, not in the foreseeable future at any rate.'

Goldman looked greatly puzzled: he hovered in front of me with one finger moving near to my face. I felt that in this mood of rare exasperation he might poke it in my eye. He seemed unable to take in my simple statement.

'Sorry,' I added, 'but it is quite definite.'

'But why?' Goldman appealed to the shelves of books behind me and two blue-rinsed mystified American ladies standing in the doorway. 'Why? All right. So now you are in the saddle. But the wheel turns, my friend ...' He went back ponderously to his seat.

'Not worth it!' A loud, typical, gratuitous remark by Goldman climaxed my bidding on a rather expensive manuscript. 'Giving gold for gold. That's what an amateur does,' he explained to his rather embarrassed neighbour. 'That's not business!' Goldman turned round to glare at me and then left the room.

I did not like Goldman, and a break with him would mean release from his aggravating, continual demonstration of superiority. But I did not really dislike him, and I thought it was silly to quarrel over nothing. I went downstairs and found him waiting to collect a payment slip. There was a crowd at the long counter, so I went up to him and pointed at a seat, half pushing him in irritation. There was no real reason why I should go into details about Margaret's financial position and I was annoyed at being jockeyed to the point of doing so.

'Look, Felix. You started worrying me about these damn books immediately Stone was dead. I told you I would see if I could get Mrs Stone to sell them to you. But the simple fact is she does not need to sell and is not going to do so. Now, is that clear? No one else is going to buy them. You haven't been squeezed out. But if they are not for sale I can't get them for you.'

He was convinced but still a little puzzled.

'That's queer,' he said. 'I don't pretend to be a mind reader but I should have said that Edward lived right up to what he made. And you know how keen a buyer he was – I thought he ploughed back his profits into more stock. He always said that good books were better than money in the bank. So she doesn't need to sell – she's quite well off?'

'So I understand.' I had come to the end of the information I was prepared to give him.

'Wait a minute,' he said, thoughtfully fingering his top lip, 'come to think of it I do remember him saying something last summer, as if he was going to come into money. We were talking about an extremely valuable book that was coming up for sale in New York and I told him it was too rich for his blood. And he said – now what was it? – ah yes: "Not after Christmas." Didn't say any more than that. I thought at the time he might be coming into some money. Must be quite a large sum if Mrs Stone can sit back and live on it.' He sighed. 'Well, that's life – he inherits money and then he dies so he can't spend it.' He looked me over carefully and put out his hand. 'Well, no hard feelings, kid. You must come out to dinner with us one evening. Sarah's cooking is the best ...'

In Bond Street I found patches of fog which thickened considerably even as I looked round for a taxi. Then I noticed how long and slow the queues of traffic were, with madly moving windscreen wipers trying futilely to clear the ominously black stuff, and decided to walk through to St Martin's Lane and sample the turbot at Sheekey's which Orville had so warmly recommended.

Afterwards, I was looking in a bookshop window in Cecil Court when I caught sight of Charlie Hayter, out of the corner of my eye. He was walking briskly through the Court, carrying a large sack, gesticulating with his free hand and laughing to himself. I heard him say, 'Manuscripts? By Christ, we'll give 'em manuscripts!' He seemed to be very pleased about something.

When I got to the entrance of the Court he had disappeared into a dense patch of fog; then I saw him vanishing into the passage by the Odeon Cinema. I followed him round Leicester Square, playing a kind of hide-and-seek. I thought I had finally lost him by the Vega Restaurant and rushed round the corner of Orange Street to practically bump into him. He was staring in the window of the caviare shop with a look of moody introspection, the bulky sack at rest on the pavement.

I stood by his side and he said without looking round, as if he had been expecting me: 'I don't know about you, Mr Seldon, but I eat mainly out of tins. Now a little of that, some Bath Oliver biscuits, a carton of raspberry-flavoured yoghourt with the top of the milk, and I'm in luxury.'

We studied the exotic tins of Bisque de Homard and Truffes de Perigord. He pointed at a box of caviarette, showing lustreless nails and rather dirty knuckles.

'I rather fancy that,' he said, breathing heavily. 'And,' he nodded slowly and rhythmically like a mechanical figure in a shop window. 'what's more to the point, I'm going to have it.

'See these.' He pointed to the sack on the pavement. 'All manuscripts of unpublished novels. The thrills and spills of the motor-cycling game. By a chap who has spent his days making jam rolls and writing at night. I went out to Sudbury to get 'em. He's never tried to place them with a publisher. Think of that – writing book after book and never seeing one in print. But we'll get them published.' He sounded unusually confident. 'That may surprise you but' – his tone was confidential as if he was letting me in on some Stock Exchange secret – 'there's a new reading bunch today. They'll eat this stuff up. Brand's Hatch, the Isle of Man, the T.T. It's all in there.' He patted the top of the sack. 'Yes, I deserve a little spread.'

He nudged me gently. 'You're a bachelor like me, Mr Seldon, I believe.' I hesitated before agreeing that my condition was as chronic as his, obliquely studying his bumpy profile and the lifeless hair, like dead grass, showing under the greasy hat. But I could see his point. Margaret had responded to me sexually, but that was because she had been starved in that way for years. We had little else in common and I could not see the attraction lasting. I was too old and unsuccessful for Kate. I nodded.

'Not much comfort in that sometimes. But I find a tasty snack is a good pick me up.' He looked round carefully and became confidential again. 'Now, those Lupin letters – were they the kind of thing that would have to be published *sub rosa*, if you get my meaning?'

'Well yes, I suppose so,' I replied. 'Some parts could not have been published in the ordinary way, but I expect they hoped to get away with printing such a small edition and distributing it privately.'

'Ah, I see – that explains it. You see, I was talking to this customer of mine – a poet.' He added the noun as if it was a significant adjective that would explain much that he had to say. 'And he said he thought this Petronius Press geezer was a young chap called Ronnie True, and that he's dead and good riddance apparently. He ran a club called the Mandragora, for hermaphrodiddles, took naughty photos of them and then blacked them. Now the bloke who told me this wants to remain anonymous, if you understand.' He winked and touched my arm with a purple hand, and added with emphasis: 'But he knows what he's talking about on that subject. Yes, this Petronius ... True was notorious, and he said there were quite a few people not too sorry when he copped it. During the war sometime. Do you mind holding this stuff while I pop in here for a moment?'

24

BLACKMAIL. The word came mysteriously into my mind during the night after my conversation with Hayter. It had been an evening when I had anticipated insomnia and had tried to evade it with my sometimes successful device of the home-made concert. I had sat up late listening to a long programme of favourite records, mixing Billie Holiday with George Malcolm playing Bach's Toccata in D, and Ella Fitzgerald with the Jupiter Symphony. At the end of it my mind was still active in a purposeless way with unformulated worries, but going into the bathroom and reaching for the bottle of sleeping tablets the sight of the pale valetudinarian face in the mirror annoyed me so much that I did not take them.

Oddly enough, I had fallen asleep within a few minutes of getting into bed. After an hour or so a car's headlight woke me with a curious shock. For a moment I lay listening, holding my breath, as if to detect someone else in the room, but then fragments of a dream gradually came together. I had been up in a giant fairground swing, the kind that goes up and over while the seat remains upright. One minute the air had been full of laughter and the blaring, mechanical roundabout music, then suddenly it had faded away and the swing had stopped. I was suspended alone in the silent cold air. When I stood up to look at the deserted fairground below, I felt trapped in the vast steel skeleton of the swing. Then a spotlight from the ground swung up into my eyes and I was conscious of someone sitting by my side, and touched a cold limp hand and heard a whisper: 'Blackmail.'

I got up and went to the window and stared at the wet road lit up from time to time by the passing cars. Watching the gusts of driving rain hitting the black puddles I took the word blackmail and realized how obvious it had been. That it had not struck me before was due to my obsession with my own interests.

I knew that True, reputed to have been a blackmailer, had suddenly come into money in 1943 when he bought the Ibiza letters. Stone had questioned in his journal whether this prosperity was sinister. In the same year True had died in mysterious circumstances, and it must have been soon after that that Stone had begun to receive the regular payment of a hundred pounds in cash each month to account for the fourteen thousand pounds he had on deposit. This made it look as if Stone knew something which enabled him to follow on in True's footsteps extorting money from Mr X.

But if that was so it in turn posed another question. If someone had killed True to stop being blackmailed, why should he then submit to it from Stone? The only explanation I could think of lay in Stone's description of True's dangerously wilful impulses. True might have become wildly greedy in his demands while Stone remained content with what was, from the victim's point of view, an expensive but bearable pension.

I shivered standing on the bare boards by the window and went back to bed, but sleep was out of the question while my mind was teased with what seemed infinite possibilities. The circumstances of Stone's death now appeared menacing. Had the motor-cyclist roared up that quiet lane on a mission to kill him? These thoughts pursued one another in an endless chain until I became quite incapable of sorting them out from a meaningless jumble, and heard my alarm bell from a dull stupor.

A shower and coffee pulled me round, but the problem was still no easier to resolve. I felt that the pattern only just eluded me, and did so because of the anomalies of behaviour. I needed more facts. I did consider Stone was capable of crime because there was a very strong amoral acquisitive strain in him, but it would have had to be on terms that he thought worth while. He would have considered it carefully, tried to rationalize the project, and to look on it as another business.

Suddenly I remembered what Goldman had told me at Sotheby's. Stone had hinted to him that he would be considerably richer by

Christmas. With this in mind I could imagine a possible sequence of events. If Stone had some evidence incriminating Mr X with True's death, he might have kept it in a bank or somewhere similarly invulnerable and blackmailed X over the years with it. Then perhaps he had decided to ask for a lump sum to surrender it: a meeting place had been fixed, of the remote kind used for the monthly payments, but instead of the lucrative interview he had hoped for the motor-cyclist had been there to kill him. This guessing was unsatisfactory as it left many gaps, but some of them were due to human infallibility. The method of killing was not dependable, as Stone had proved by surviving the blow. X had therefore taken a big gamble – one that tended to show that Stone's demands had become as intolerable as those made by True.

On my way to my office I was able at last to put these questions out of my mind as I felt that solution to some of them might be waiting for me at Hurley that afternoon. After my encounter with Hayter I had gone to the G.P.O. in Trafalgar Square and found a phone number listed for Mrs Violet True, still at the address given at her son's inquest. A confused phone call had resulted in her agreeing to see me. I had told her vaguely that 'I was interested in Mr True's work'. I had got the Grosvenor Street Car Co. to let me have a Bristol 403 on trial for the afternoon. I felt that I was all set to untangle the mystery of True and Stone, and perhaps to find the Lupin letters. It was quite possible that they still reposed in a drawer at Victoria Villa, Hurley. In my mind I composed a succinct cable to Orville stating that the letters were in my possession, and decided to split the £500 with Mrs True.

While June was occupied in sending out statements, I went into the tiny room we used for packing and tea-making. June hated that room; although it was as narrow as a passage, it contained a wash basin, large rolls of string and corrugated card and piles of paper, so that one had to squeeze through to the packing bench. A white elephant in the form of an enormous, gilt-framed, Burne-Jones oil painting filled the other wall. She disliked packing, too, and demonstrated it effectively by refusing to master the simple knack of making an adequate parcel and secure knot. But I was quite happy to leave her to the tedious accounts and be engaged in the nearly mindless occupation of wrapping paper and folding card.

The small window faced a blank brick wall, but I escaped from the grimy view and conjured up the afternoon when I had walked down to the sea with Kate. In retrospect that afternoon with her had a lyrical quality, the images a *hokku*-like intensity, and certainly I had never found anyone with whom I was more quickly at ease. But I knew that I always enjoyed looking back on things more than actually doing them. My inability to enjoy the present seemed to me my biggest defect. I wondered if I was doomed always to slide through situations, not making the most of them, and then spend hours thinking about them. The reason for all this semi-philosophic speculation was my lack of success with Kate. I wanted badly to see her again but could think of no way of doing so.

From the office I heard June murmur something and then the high fluting voice of a young man replying, 'Actually, yes. But I don't choose books – they choose me.'

It was the kind of voice I associated with Universities and conversations carried out at long distance across rooms for effect. As I left, I saw the tight cavalry twill trousers, heard him say something improbable about collecting Proust manuscripts, and went out quickly to pick up the Bristol.

25

SPEEDING ALONG the Bath road, I noticed an occasional patch of fog reluctant to disperse under the feeble warmth of the sun, set low in the pale sky like a white coin. And when I turned off past the Maidenhead Thicket and went down by the golf course, I could see fields covered with a thick grey mist a few inches deep which made them look like mysterious lakes.

Victoria Villa was shrouded from the damp lane that led to it by a dense copse. There was a badly verdigrised copper name-plate on the wooden gate and the garden had run wild. Briars hung across what had once been a lawn, conquered by couch grass and cow-parsley; the remains of a gravel path was full of ground elder. The red bricks of the house were partly hidden by the scaffolding of a decayed magnolia. Some enthusiast, perhaps fifty years before, had indulged in a craze for seeing how many bushes and trees could be grown there; now they dominated the house and gave it a shunned aspect. An ancient yew in the lane and two giant macrocarpas kept out the light. The atmosphere was chilly and still. To the left I could see the crumbling remains of an octagonal summer-house, of an earlier date than the villa, with grey walls elaborately moulded under the lichen.

As I went up the path I had to duck under a massive forsythia bush in order to avoid walking through knee-deep wet weeds; even so the long trailing branches flicked across my head, scattering a shower of drops on my back. I pushed more of them aside with a sense of *déjà vu*, and suddenly remembered the intransigent bush in Stone's garden. A bold, orange-beaked blackbird, rooting among the rubbishy old magnolia leaves by the door, eyed me carefully but did not move as I reached for the knocker fretted with rust like a delicate fungus.

I knocked twice and then heard a tap-tapping noise. When the door opened, a tiny smoke-grey kitten rushed out and a woman took a step backwards into the dark hall and looked up at me with her body bent over at a right angle from the waist. She held a short stick and I realized that her normal posture when standing or walking would be twisted like that. This miserable condition induced a qualm of conscience for bothering her with what might well be a wild goose chase, but she beckoned me in quite cheerfully. Her large dark brown eyes had a youthful brightness.

'I do hope you won't find the house unbearably gloomy – it is at its worst on a day like this. All those trees ...' She gestured hopelessly.

We made our way slowly along a passage and into a small living-room made bright by a coal fire.

'Now, tell me what particular aspect of my husband's work interests you,' she said, pointing with her stick to the wall by the fireplace which was covered with photographs in gilt frames.

'I'm afraid I could not have made myself clear on the phone the other day. It is your son's work I wanted to ask about.'

'My son's work!' She mused on that for a moment. 'If I say *what* work, I hope you won't think I mean it in a slighting way. But he accomplished so little. Many talents, all squandered, alas. You mean his photography? I should have thought he was not very well known. Whereas his father ...'

'Those photographs are by your husband?'

'Yes, Gilbert was quite famous as a theatrical photographer. That's how I met him – I was at the Royal Court under Vedrenne and Barker. But Ronnie could not stick at it. He had a lyrical impulse, an eye for composition; but what good is that without discipline, hard work? My husband was one of the first photographers to make strips of little films, rather like Polyphotos nowadays, of scenes during rehearsals, and they were used by producers in planning the final *mise-en-scène*. Granville Barker's stage directions were very elaborate and detailed, you know. The idea of such painstaking work would have appalled Ronnie. He wanted to create a masterpiece at the first shot.'

She was staring across the room at her husband's work and I was able to study her unobtrusively. She wore a dark blue woollen suit with a gentian blouse and black lizard shoes. The skin of her neck was thin and transparent. Veins showed in the backs of her hands like blue worms, and her face was a patchwork of tiny lines, but the eyes that looked out from it were those of a young girl. Time had played cruel tricks with her, but I could tell that she had once been a very attractive woman.

'I know hardly anything about photography,' I admitted. 'It was some literary work that your son embarked on, editing and publishing some letters of Frederick Lupin.'

'Letters!' she said doubtfully. 'I've never heard of them. When was this?'

'About 1943.' Any question or remark I could make seemed to be linked with a morbid interest in her son's fate.

She frowned: 'I saw very little of him at that time. He came here occasionally, but he lived in London ... You know he died that year?'

'Yes, I knew a friend of his, Edward Stone, and it was through him I learnt about the letters.'

'You're sure of this – I mean that he actually did anything about them? He had so many projects that came to nothing.'

'I'm sure he worked at it – I've seen a prospectus he issued.'

'Really? Well, I'm learning something about my own son today. I'm glad I answered your phone call. I don't always, you know. Sometimes I just let it ring. So often bad news ... And my little book of phone numbers – the last time I looked through it I thought, "Dead, dead, dead!"'

Needles jabbed into my leg and I looked down to see the blue-grey kitten with celadon eyes hanging there. I picked it up and Mrs True smiled again. I sensed that we were sympathetic and that I should have no trouble in persuading her to show me her son's papers. There was no need to push the matter.

She moved to the window and I joined her, looking out over the tangled wet grass and brown iris leaves at the tottering wreck of a two-storied boathouse.

'You should have seen that when we came here. All gleaming white and green paint. It was my husband's dream – a house by

112

the river. Perhaps *The Wind in the Willows* was to blame! And then he was fascinated by that old summerhouse. I expect you noticed it. What twists fate hides from us!' She grimaced wryly.

'We came here in 1912. Such a different world! We had a brougham from Marlow, and I remember we had been to Ranelagh the previous day.' She picked up a green bowl of white hyacinths from the window ledge and impulsively thrust the flowers so close to my face that my nose struck the quivering crisp bells and I was caught momentarily in a web of scent as heavy as a drug. 'Simple pleasures,' she murmured, 'that's all I live for now.'

She stroked the kitten as it nestled high on my lapel. Her fingers were slender but the knuckles were grotesquely swollen.

'My life has been so completely different in its various phases that sometimes I feel that I have lived a number of separate lives. In 1910 for instance – my husband's work had a particular vogue then – "the doyen of his craft", Vedrenne said – and we spent most of the year travelling round Europe ...'

As she spoke I could imagine her quite vividly, alighting from a carriage in Biarritz, the fragile face and big eyes peeping out from under a huge hat, strolling along the Promenade des Anglais, punctuating picture postcards with capital letters and exclamation marks in violet ink, dressing up in elaborate Charles Ricketts costumes, clinging to her husband's arm as they entered the Théâtre Antoine.

'Yes, in 1910, and later than that, until the holocaust began in 1914, the world seemed full of infinite opportunities. One sees that one must perforce be blind at that stage to the basic sadness of life – it is the time for optimism. Later on, we were not quite so well off, my husband had to turn to ordinary photography – weddings, children, that kind of thing. And in the twenties and thirties we led a routine suburban life, bringing up Ronnie ... And now – well, I just wait, though I don't know for what. I think it was Rabelais who said, "For the Great Perhaps".'

She leant on my arm as we went to the door. 'We'll do a little exploring, but you'll find it horribly cold and damp. I can keep this room reasonably warm and I live in it. But the rest of the house is impossible.'

26

WHEN I closed the door behind us and we walked down the passage I realized she had not exaggerated. I could not remember, since the war, being in a building so unpleasantly saturated with chilling damp. There were large ominous marks on the wallpaper and it was peeling in places. The smell of decay was rank. Moving at her crippled pace towards the dark stairs was like entering a tomb. If it had been arthritis that had bent Mrs True's spine like a taut bow, then this house was the worst possible place for her to live. She answered my unspoken question.

'It's a terror, I know, but remember that this is about the worst time of the year. Besides, I could not leave. Gilbert adored this place. And I love the village. Did you notice the church?'

'Yes, I drove up to it. And there's an interesting old building facing it, too.'

'Oh, that's the Priory. You must come again in finer weather – when explorations can be pleasant.'

We had stopped on a landing on the first floor and looked out at a curve of the river glinting faintly between the trees. She was breathing heavily. 'Gilbert died when Ronnie was only fourteen. That was probably the root of the trouble ...' She seemed to assume I knew something of her son's curious career. 'What a responsibility we parents have. Impulsiveness in my character was not for me a handicap. Some people seemed to like it! But in Ronnie it became wilful, distorted. It ruined his life. And it came from me! Remorse is the most painful of human feelings, I think.'

I tried hard to think of something meaningful yet comforting to say, but without success. Going along a corridor she pointed with her stick: 'There are some rooms I dare not enter. Too full of memories.'

The journey upstairs and back into the past which I was subjecting her to was difficult and cruel, and I made a half-hearted effort to stop her. 'Perhaps we should forget the idea.'

'No,' she said firmly. 'You have travelled from London, and there are only a few more stairs. Besides, if anything can come from Ronnie's work I shall be glad. And the room he used for scribbling is not like one of the bedrooms. Just a place where we kept cases and things.'

She sighed deeply and looked round and up into my face. 'Gilbert had a terrible accident in that summerhouse he loved so much. He used it as a workshop and he was cleaning something with petrol ... Somehow it caught fire. Ronnie heard his screams and found him dying. He never got over the shock.'

I put a hand on her thin bony shoulder and held it a moment. She went on in a toneless voice: 'It wounded him, deep down, forever. After that he was – well, kind of dead inside. It was funny – strangers thought he was happy-go-lucky, carefree. Really it was something quite different – the opposite, in fact. The loss of all feeling.'

The top floor landing was cluttered with boxes full of photographs and large ones were piled along the walls. There were innumerable buff studies of actresses, looking yearningly over bare shoulders at the camera, smiling provocatively, a few in poses that would have been considered 'daring'. *Vanitas, vanitatum.*

Mrs True opened a door apprehensively and gestured vaguely: 'That's a rather fine mirror, but it watched me, like a spy, as I got old and bent. So I banished it here!' She smiled mischievously, and momentarily I saw her again as a delightful ingénue – all eyes in a pointed face. 'I shall leave you here while I make tea. You may find things in a muddle. This house was burgled during the war – ransacked from top to bottom. But I never could discover that anything had been taken. Probably there was nothing of sufficient value.'

Apart from the cases she had mentioned, the room was relatively bare with a cheap-looking schoolboy's desk isolated in the middle and amateurish white-painted bookshelves along one wall.

115

I switched on a shadeless light hanging over the desk and saw the bare branches of an ash tree outlined against the window. Some twigs were tapping on the glass like impatient fingers. I glanced along the books and found it was an uninteresting motley collection with a few Nineties poets in warped vellum bindings. On the mantelpiece there was a cemetery of flies, a Julia Cameron photograph of Tennyson, a chipped bust of blind Homer, and a small reproduction of Michelangelo's 'David' disguised by dust.

When I had opened the drawers in the desk I suspected that Mrs True was wrong in thinking that the burglar had not taken anything. The large one across the knee-hole and two others were bare apart from thick grey dust like wool and weightless transparent spider bodies. Another small drawer at the bottom contained only some sheets of unused purple blotting-paper – but as I closed it I heard something being scrunched at the back by this movement. I pulled the drawer right out from the grooves and discovered a small photograph which had fallen down and was bent in half at a right angle.

It showed Ronald True, seated in a cane chair, in tight black trousers and a white shirt with a Byronic furled collar open low down on his thin chest. He had a silly, self-conscious look. Simpering, I thought with distaste. Behind him, standing, with his hands lightly but possessively on True's shoulders, was James Saul. He had one eyebrow very slightly raised, otherwise his cold, unlined face was expressionless. Sitting like that, True reminded me of a ventriloquist's dummy: an evil one who might try to rebel against his master.

I turned the photograph over. There was no imprint of the 'Mandragora Studios' which I had expected, but it was inscribed in green ink, in a nervous pointed hand, 'Half Moon Street. Yester-night.'

Staring at True's face I heard myself say, 'Poor fool.' It was an inadequate attempt at an epitaph on this antinomian driven by feelings as natural to him as the normal sexual impulse was to the mass. I knew that someone like Orville could pick holes in my reasoning for finding the photograph unpleasant. I remembered, too, that True's crazy pattern of life had probably been fixed by the

116

traumatic experience of his father's terrible death. Nevertheless my involuntary exclamation summed up my true reaction: I was repelled by True's dreamy, foolish look, his attempt to be something other than a man.

I put the photograph back where it had been and went downstairs. I knew now that I should not find the Ibiza letters in the True household. I was convinced that they would have been removed with all other papers that might be incriminating, on the orders of Sir James Saul. I had a number of regrets, one of them being that I could not give a cheque to the charming and sensitive cripple who was waiting for me downstairs.

'No luck?' she asked as I went into her cosy sanctuary. The table was laid and she was preparing some hot buttered toast.

'I'm afraid not. And I feel terribly guilty about bothering you. Perhaps I can make amends by coming down one day in the spring and clearing some of that undergrowth. The ivy on the ash tree at the back keeps out a lot of light, too.'

'Would you? That would be nice.' She looked out of the window. 'There was a time when I luxuriated in being by myself. On misty days like this, particularly in the autumn, I loved to walk in those *terrains vagues* between here and Temple, and the Low Grounds near Bisham Abbey. I thought then that I lived for reverie and for things that fed it. Now, alas, when I am alone all the time, I realize it was an illusion ... Do you like quince jam?'

'Love it. Is it far to Bisham Abbey?'

'It's on the other side of the river, but if you went back through Marlow you would pass Bisham church – that is where Ronnie was buried. The churchyard is often flooded in the winter, but it is a wonderful setting, right on the river bank ...'

By the time I got to Bisham it was too dark to read the lettering on the stones, and I did not discover which was True's grave; but I sat for a few minutes on a wooden seat looking out over the black fast-moving river to the dank and deserted fields on the other side. I heard some dragging footsteps on the gravel path but no one appeared. I felt unreal, 'a spectre amid spectres'. The lonely music of the river emphasized my sense of solitude.

Thinking of True's death, I remembered a German soldier I had seen floating in the River Sangro, maintained in an upright position by a balancing effect of his equipment and pack and the brushwood his arms were tangled in. Looking down on his dirty matted hair bobbing up and down just beneath the surface it had seemed possible that he might still be alive, but a swirl of the current had tilted him backwards to show a grey, pulpy swollen face with ragged holes in it. I could visualize True's body, looking much like that, haphazardly swimming in on a high tide, but I was certain now that his death had not been accidental and I doubted if he was alive when he was put in the sea. A hectic scene between him and Saul, ending in a murderous blow, was more likely. Possibly in the Folly, the 'super studio' that Kate had pointed out to me, which had since been allowed to fall derelict. Then the *fauxnaif* would have been dumped with the other flotsam in Poole Harbour with the knowledge that some days in the sea would disguise the fatal wound.

My quest for the Lupin letters had been a useless one in most ways, but it had brought me into contact with Kate. My suspicions about Saul's guilt were strong, but they were flimsily based and probably impossible to prove. I knew that I should not take them to the police when it was unlikely that anything would be achieved apart from hurting Kate. As I left the churchyard I felt as though I was trying to shrug off ghosts.

27

DURING THE week after my trip to Hurley I had some rather irritating phone calls but none of the depressing kind which haunted Mrs True. One was from a printer confronting me with the unpleasant fact that the costs of reproducing an illuminated manuscript and a *trompe l'oeil* painting in my next catalogue would be more than I could pay. Another very long call was from a customer in Bath who was dissatisfied with the packing on a book we had sent him. It had reached him in a 'deplorable' state, but he would not return the book and went on and on about the inadequacy of the parcel, vehemently urging me to 'take this up with the packing department'. By the end of the call I had idly looked through my desk drawer and come on a leaflet of chess rules that had been in a travelling set Ben Meyer had given me at Christmas.

I had known the rules of chess since I was a schoolboy, but now I could read a secondary meaning into them and I studied them again after I had replaced the receiver.

The Game

The objective in the game is to play the various pieces in such a way as to 'checkmate' the opponent's King, that is, place the opposing King in a position to be taken, with no move open to escape from that position or no piece to intercept between itself and the attacking piece, and thus remove the 'check'.

Sir James Saul could certainly be regarded as the guileful black King: then Stone became a white pawn moving haplessly straight ahead in a blind effort to reach the 8th rank, but obliterated by a black pawn *en passant*. Berning plainly was one of the black Knights: 'The Knight's move is a little puzzling to beginners ... his move is a leap.' I was particularly struck by the aptness of another note: 'The King may take a piece but not be taken.'

If one wanted to hit out at Saul then the first essential was to recognize the strength of his position, entrenched at the back of the board, surrounded by expendable pawns, Rooks, Knights and Bishops. The police were not likely even to consider acting on the True case, when the death had been one by drowning in 1943. Stone's murder was a very different matter, but even so it was obvious that Saul was indeed the King. Was it conceivable that he could be brought to trial for a crime committed in England while he had been lying seriously ill in Switzerland? Even if the motor-cyclist could be found, and there would be nothing to link him with Stone, establishing that Saul had been behind the murder would probably be impossible. Undoubtedly he would have given his decision to some shadowy figure not in this country who would have passed it to the Knight Berning. The black pawn would have known only what he had to do and how much he would be paid to do it.

Action against Saul, to be effective, would have to be subtle. The only way I could think of was by trying to frighten him with a resurrected Ronnie True in the form of compromising letters signed R.B.T. Threats from a dead man would be a form of danger that even Saul would find difficult to handle. Whether they would have much effect was another matter. I remembered that Kate had told me of her father's succinct comment on the quotation from Herodotus carved over the doorway of T. E. Lawrence's cottage. Cloud's Hill was only a few miles from Splay and they had been there several times. On one occasion he had translated Hippoclides' comment as 'I don't care', adding, 'Only a man who cared would bother to carve that.' It seemed to me that Saul was one of those few people who really don't care and thereby become basically impervious. And the idea of the threatening letters did not appeal to me much – it was only another form of blackmail, though not for money. I tried to justify my not doing anything about Saul on several scores – one of them being that Kate had told me that his heart attack had been serious and was likely to recur.

I had an intriguing and quite exciting phone call at the end of the week, late on the Friday afternoon, just after June had left. Someone who did not give his name said he was phoning on Kate Saul's behalf and asked me to meet her at a party. When I asked where and when he said it was 'quite close' and offered to pick me up 'any time after six-thirty'. 'Fancy dress,' he said, adding very quickly, 'that is for some – you need not bother, of course. I expect you would like to be called for in Mayfair. Our car ...'

'But wouldn't Kate like me to pick her up somewhere? I could get a taxi ...'

'Our car,' he repeated patiently, 'will be going down Regent Street about seven. O.K.?'

'Yes, all right, seven – outside Martinez.'

'Martin who?'

'Martinez – a restaurant in Swallow Street, narrow little street past Austin Reed's, going down to Piccadilly Circus.'

He said fine, but sounded vague. 'What will you be wearing – just so they'll know you? The car is a black Humber.'

'Dark grey suit, dark blue tie, white mac,' I specified, puzzled by the idea that I should need identification outside Martinez.

'Fine – see you later, then.' I got another sentence started with 'But, I say ...' when he rang off.

I had two double finos in Martinez, admired the tiles and ate quite a number of olives in case the party did not materialize. When I went to the entrance on the chime of seven I did not expect the car to turn up. I felt that the call might have been some kind of feeble joke – there was something weird about the man who phoned, as if he had been taught to issue an invitation but not to deal with any unexpected queries it might set off. However, the car – a large powerful sombre machine – was there, practically blocking the street. There was a fat man in the driver's seat, and a small man wearing a narrow top hat, with two girls, at the back.

The driver, in tight navy roll-neck pullover and serge trousers, opened the door and stuttered a welcome: 'Th-thanks for being on time, Mac. It's a hard b-bus to park here.'

'Move, Sailor, move,' said the man at the back in a nervous staccato Brooklyn accent. 'Let's get this show on the road.'

The fat man fumbled around with the gear lever and said with a delicate plaintiveness, 'Take it easy, Lenny.'

Slowly we moved off down Swallow Street and then jerked out into Piccadilly. It was apparent that Sailor was a terrible driver who compromised with our practice of driving on the left hand side of the road by keeping strictly in the middle, and his concentration was not helped by Lenny bouncing about on the back seat, leaning forward suddenly and continually shouting advice and insults: 'You've slipped your clutch. Make this dragster move! Vee-boom!'

Lenny had enough energy to make up for the apathy and quietness of his female companions, both of whom wore fancy dresses designed to show décolletage and leg. They had their coats hung loosely round their shoulders and shrank back in the corners of the seat to give Lenny plenty of room. In the light from Regent Street, which Sailor turned back into with terrific verve, they looked ghastly. They wore too much powder and their lipsticks were so pale as to appear white, but there was obviously something else wrong. Lenny appeared aware of this at times, and in between asking them to have another drink from his flask he studied one of them fixedly, tapping her on the knee and pleading, 'Come on, Natalie, eh? Snap out of it – you don't want to be a pill at the party, do you?' He was dressed in a shabby Uncle Sam outfit with a silk stars-and-stripes waistcoat. He leaned forward and began to dance some intricate steps while still seated, clicking his fingers, singing snatches of songs, whistling and humming. He ignored me completely.

We were going up Regent Street fairly fast and crossed one set of traffic lights as the red flashed on. I concentrated on the road and asked the driver. 'Where's the party? Near here?'

'There you have me, Mac,' he said out of the side of his mouth, quietly as though he did not want Lenny to hear. 'I know we go up Regent, down Oxford and then B-Bayswater – I don't know the rest of them funny names; but I can get you there, yes, sir. Once I've been to a place I never forget.' We were still near the middle of the road, causing panic to pedestrians on islands.

'Come, come, come!' said Lenny, leaning forward and snapping his fingers on either side of Sailor's head. 'Faster, man! Natalie's not so good. Are you going to be sick, Natalie?'

Natalie was silent, but heaved significantly and her distress was communicated to the rest of us. Lenny gave her arm a shake: 'You can't be sick here!' But there was not much conviction in his tone and his banter subsided as we sped down Oxford Street and whizzed round Marble Arch, scattering taxi cabs on either side of us like pins in a bowling alley.

Sailor kept looking at Natalie in the driving mirror and increasing his speed. I recognized Queensway Station but then I was lost in a tangle of small streets. Sailor did not falter, though he often went round corners on the wrong side of the road. He negotiated a complicated arrangement of turns with enormous panache and hardly any braking, and then swirled to a stop in front of some other cars by an alley-way.

'This is it,' he said as I jerked violently towards the windscreen and then back into my seat. The three in the rear had been jumbled up a bit during the last figure of eight movement executed by the Humber. I got out quickly and waited for them. Natalie was first, hugging her coat round her, and walked off down the road. Lenny followed her.

'Can I do anything?' I said to him, pointing at Natalie.

'Do you mind?' he replied in an angry voice. He gestured towards the alley with his thumb. 'What's up, Doc? We brought you right to the door, didn't we? Now get off my back!'

I shrugged my shoulders as he went off, followed by Sailor and the other girl. 'The party is here?' I shouted to the fat man.

'Can't you see the open door?' he shouted back, adopting Lenny's aggressive tone.

I went up the alley. It looked like a mews that had been turned into garages with flats above. Dim light came from one half-open door and there was a polyphonic murmur of music, voices and faint laughter.

The doorway led straight on to steep stairs. When I peered inside I could hear the tune quite clearly: it was Glenn Miller's 'Moonlight Serenade' – one that was full of wartime memories, AFN, canteen dances and moonlit nights in Rome, for me. But the momentary spell of it was broken as I went up the stairs, noticing the white-framed gouaches by Severini of clowns and broken guitars, mandolins and deserted buildings, wondering who it was that Kate knew here and if she would be waiting for me, or whether I should feel as out of place as I had done on the way with Sailor. The record stopped and was replaced by Teddy Wilson's 'Don't blame me'.

28

At the top of the stairs the lime green carpet continued along a passage-way to a brightly lit room full of people and smoke. The white wall on the left hand side was decorated with prints of exotic birds. There were four doors in the dark green wall on my right, one open to disclose a chaotic kitchen.

Three people formed an unenthusiastic welcoming committee near the door. A tall, bored-looking man, dressed as a Mounty, held himself bent back as if to withdraw from the smoke-filled air, the hubbub, and life in general. A ginger haired man pushed a glass and a bottle of sparkling white wine at me. His was a face I thought I imperfectly remembered, from a brush in a car showroom in Warren or Great Portland Street. He had a cultivated level look, and tiny, eye-beguiling, red veins round his nose. The woman was small with bright blue bullace eyes, skimpy blonde hair and a moody mouth.

The welcome consisted of, 'Champers, Squire?' from the car salesman and vague nods from the other two. I drifted past them into the swirling, shouting crowd. The music stopped again and I noticed a young girl, in Pierrette costume, fiddling indecisively with a pile of records.

There was a slight pressure on my arm and I found the tiny blonde with the disenchanted expression standing by me. She regarded me with eyebrows dramatically arched to convey puzzlement, holding her face cupped in her right hand, supporting her right elbow with her left palm. All this theatrical stuff was rather cramped and spoiled by the press of people around us. In particular, there was a hefty man dressed as a clown, with two amber pustules pushing through the floury surface of his cheek, who wavered and side-stepped quite gently, on our feet.

'I do *know* you – you're my husband's friend, Jeff Warner ... ?' said the blonde, her voice trailing off doubtfully.

'I'm afraid not. I'm a complete impostor here. In fact, I should hand back this drink and leave,' I said.

'Certainly *not*. Of course *you* know Hugh.' She had an odd way of emphasizing words and a repertoire of dramatic expressions that made me think she might have been on the stage. Conversation with her was like taking part in a third-rate pantomime.

'No – I don't, I'm sorry to say. The terrible thing is I don't know whose party this is. I just came as someone invited me over the phone and said a friend of mine, Kate Saul, would be here.'

'Well, how *odd*.' She regarded me blankly for a moment and then switched on a mysterious smile. 'I don't know anyone called Saul and *this* is my party. Never mind – we'll ask Hugh.' She indicated the Mounty.

The girl in the corner had apparently asked for advice as to which record to play and everyone called out titles. Hugh's wife shouted, 'Sinatra singing "Bim, *Bam*, Baby".' She punched me gently in the chest and said, 'Now you like that, don't you, *Bim*, Bam, Baby.' A tough-looking Australian laughed maniacally and called out a suggestion which sounded obscene. But when the record came on it was some South American number and the blonde guided me into the slow-moving centre of the room. The Australian made a threesome of our dance by holding the blonde's shoulders for a moment but she got rid of him with a brief whispered comment.

'So you don't know a soul ... ?' she asked in a silly, little-girl voice. When she forgot her range of vivacious expression her face relapsed into the fixed depressed look of someone who is tired and drunk but trying to appear sober. She had moulded her hard sexless body to mine so that every movement of my legs touched hers. 'Not anyone?' she insisted.

'Well, I thought I had met your friend at the door, but only on business somewhere, and I'm not sure about that.'

'Weirdsville – I mean, *really* arcane, dahling,' she murmured. 'You come to a party and you don't *know* who's giving it or who invited you. A likely tale!' Her hand was tight round the back of my neck and her fingers were strong. She relaxed her grip to pinch my ear. 'You're a naughty boy.'

She appeared to have forgotten about interrogating her husband who still stood, in this world but not of it, at the door. He peered unsmilingly from under the big Mounty hat and looked as if his boots were hurting him. His expression was world weary, as if he remembered a hundred parties like this and despaired of finding pleasure in another one. His wife looked up into my face and gave a practised vamp smile.

'This I must get to the *bottom* of, dahling,' she said, breathing a mixture of gin and peppermint toothpaste right into my nose. But it was not to be. As she said it an amiable little woman, in Charlie Chaplin clobber, took her arms and whispered something. I just caught the words, 'The children can't sleep.'

'Flipping kids,' said Hugh's wife. She pointed at me as she went off. 'Don't go away. *This* must be investigated exhaustively ...'

For some moments I had had a feeling that I was being watched and as I made my way back to the wall I saw who it was. An extremely tall and bulky man in a light grey flannel suit and bright foulard tie was studying me with a malevolent expression. When I looked at him his hooded green eyes glanced away and then back, his mouth twisted in a shrewd grin, showing lots of small, even teeth. There was something very unpleasant about this brief exchange of looks. He turned his back to me but the impression of too many teeth cramped into a wolfish and contemptuous expression remained.

I was rapidly becoming fed up with the party. I did not mind waiting if Kate would eventually appear, but dancing with Hugh's wife was a pleasure I would sooner do without, and that seemed to be the only way in which inquiries about Kate would be conducted.

A man wearing a bad imitation of an old-fashioned policeman's uniform, undone at the collar, was propped up between a sofa and the wall. He stared about glassily and then gave me a fatuous smile: 'I'm happy. Why don't you try to be happy?' I decided to get another drink and hear about hard times in Warren Street but the dispenser of wine had disappeared. As I pushed through to the door my arm was taken firmly by a pimply husky youth in a dark blue blazer and striped tie: 'You're wanted in the hall ...'

I asked who wanted me but he just nodded and slipped through the dancers. The Australian got hold of my lapel: 'Quit mousing about with my sheila.'

I passed the vigilant Hugh, who was still looking infinitely bored, and breathed relatively fresh air. As I did so a heavy foot ground down on the back of my heel. I turned and saw the giant in the grey flannel suit, smiling, eyebrows raised in an unspoken question. There was no one in the hall but I could hear a noise from one of the other rooms. It was a bedroom and Hugh's wife was bent over, talking to a small figure sitting in bed behind a barricade of women's coats. She looked up and said to me, 'Oh, don't go, dahling.'

I felt a jarring push in my side that took me a long way towards the stairs. I half turned to see the big chap coming up behind me and then another push caught me off balance and I fell down the stairs taking a picture with me, landing in a heap with it at the bottom. There was a taste of salt in my mouth. The tall minatory figure hung over me as I tried to get my breath and think straight. It seemed that I had given offence, in some unknown way, to this huge lunatic.

He narrowed his eyes and said slowly, 'I'm going to hurt you, sonny.' His face remained quite calm. He pulled on a pair of pigskin gloves. Farther up the stairs two other men were watching this curious scene. I saw one of them rubbing his nose with excitement. On the edge of the landing the ginger haired car salesman looked down and said, 'What's going on? Now stop that.' One of the two spectators turned to him and said, 'Shut your mucking mouth, mate.'

The big man moved down and pulled me up by my lapels, handling my six foot and thirteen stone body as if I were a child. 'This is a pleasure,' he said quietly. 'It bloody is. I don't like your type.'

Physical defence seemed hopeless and I thought that reason might prevail. 'But why ... ?' I asked vainly. He made a short jab with his right fist which winded me and took me grovelling to the floor. That one blow, in which his hand had travelled a foot, had made my ribs ache and jarred my head as though it had been struck with a truncheon. He moved slowly down. I spun round on the floor like a mechanical toy unable to right itself, scrambled up and dashed off into the dark. From the stairs there was a confusion of voices. Someone was saying, 'Look here, look here,' in a tone of mild annoyance.

As I went through the door another thump, in the back of my neck, made me stagger a bit. But the night air hit my face like cold water, and the alley-way stones sounded hollow under my flying feet. My mac was on the ottoman in the hall at the flat, but all I could think of was putting distance between me and the grey-suited maniac.

Following shouts echoed down the street as I reached the parked cars. Round a corner I paused for a second and then went through a narrow passage-way. I cleared a brick wall at the end like an inspired hurdler – the memory of that meaty fist mashing my neck was all the encouragement I needed.

At the next corner I paused again, with my heart thumping like an engine, and heard the sound of several pairs of feet pounding through the passage. I went into the small front garden of a semi-detached house, and tried the side gate. It was locked so I scrambled over it and fell on my shins with a jolt that took most of the breath out of me. I barged into a dustbin and then whirled round and was nearly decapitated by a clothes line supporting one flapping sheet. With aching calf muscles I sprinted to the end of the narrow garden, ploughing through a pile of dirt and over a rotten fence. Leaping another low wall I dropped much further on the other side and found myself in a concrete area, in the shadow of a block of flats.

Beyond a high fence I could hear an express train screaming past and a series of jarring noises from shunting carriages. Then there was a sharp expletive as someone fell over the wall near me. A man picked himself up, grabbing his knees momentarily, and then pounced on me, shouting, 'Right, Des. He's here!' He got in some professional blows to my ribs and kidneys but I hit him with a right cross that crunched satisfactorily into his nose and made it bleed. We began to wrestle in a very amateurish, heavy-breathing, fashion, the silence only broken by him saying optimistically, 'Get stuffed.'

It was not the giant, and we were fairly evenly matched. By the gilt buttons and his striped tie I knew it was the youth who had got me into the hall. Apparently he was content just to keep me until Des could do the punishing work. I pulled down on both of his ears and stamped very hard on one foot, and he released me.

I went round the corner of the flat and had to be content with walking on lifeless legs. I climbed yet one more wall, with my arms aching and hands shaking. Somewhere in my mind I was rehearsing what I would say if I could find someone to whom I could appeal for help: anything I could think of sounded ludicrously dramatic or feeble. The sounds of following footsteps were broken up with confused shouts and what sounded like a running fight. There was an enormous building in front of me and an unpleasant chemical smell, distinct, but one which I could not identify.

I looked up at the top of the building and realized instantly what the odd smell was – I was in a gasworks. I knew then that somewhere I should find men working, and felt that any group of sane people would automatically bring this mad chase to an end. I ran round the gasometer, seeing a string of overhead lights off to the left. I sped on hopefully, but my footsteps were dogged by others gaining on me and I panicked a bit, running too quickly in the semi-darkness, cannoning from a rail into some kind of gantry, and then found I was ploughing my way upwards, my feet slipping uselessly from under me. I was floundering about on a great mound of coal. I tried to get up it by taking great steps as if on a giant staircase, but I slipped down a little way and a hand came on to my ankle and started to twist. I turned on my knees and at Lautrec-height began to swop blows with the persistent youth who was standing, balanced precariously, below me. I was better placed and got in two punishing blows to his face and toppled him over backwards. He went down in an avalanche of coal.

There was a small group of men, with the giant Des in the middle, fighting at the bottom of the pile. This puzzled me greatly but it was a mystery I could not investigate. I went up and up the hill of coal, scrabbling a way through it. I clawed, tasted, breathed and smelt coal till I got to the top, and a lunge took me over the other side, tobogganing quite slowly down, with my arms out in front like a cautious child on a playground slide. At the bottom I found myself in a path between two great mounds and it led me to a boundary fence that I climbed as slowly as a cripple.

29

I FOUND I was in Harvist Road, and at the corner of Kilburn High Road a cruising taxi picked me up and sped to Ealing without a question or comment about my weird appearance. I huddled in the dark back seat, rather like an injured cat, gingerly tracing the area of pain on my neck. Cuts in my forehead and a gravelly graze on my cheek had dried, but my left ankle hurt and seemed to be sprained.

As I had time to think about my encounter with Des I became convinced that it was not the result of having accidentally antagonized him. The gilt-buttoned youth had got me into the hall to a plan, and it had only misfired because he and his companion had stood watching as Des began his methodical attack, instead of going to the bottom of the stairs or into the mews alley to cut off my retreat. The use of Kate's name in the invitation to the party puzzled me, until I suddenly thought that Berning might have been behind this mysterious business. He was the only person who was both aware that I knew Kate and capable of planning it, but his possible reasons eluded me.

When I arrived home I negotiated the hall with great care. Mrs Maple who owned the house would only have complicated matters with her concern, and I might have dripped blood on her carpet.

As I looked into the wardrobe mirror a ludicrous figure peered out. My face was patchily black and a fringe of sooty hair was stuck to my forehead with sweat and blood. There were two long slits in my trousers and one coat pocket had been torn away. I took a shower and at first streams of black and red ran down; but by the time the water was running cool it was also clear. When I had finished there were some tiny clean fragments of coal, like freshly panned nuggets, on the white porcelain by my toes. The long soaking left me refreshed, and despite the pain of my aching neck I was surprised to diagnose an odd elation.

'Self-absorption equals futilitarianism,' Ben Meyer had said, rather smugly, to me once. It was an accurate appraisal of my condition but it lacked a cure; it was like telling a man without legs that walking is excellent exercise. Now I was beginning to wonder if anything that 'took me out of myself', as Mrs Maple would have put it, was the answer. Perhaps – for my psychological type – being chased through Kensal Green Gasworks was mainly therapeutic.

I had hoped to go to work on Saturday morning, but when I woke my ankle was too painful so I hobbled downstairs and told Mrs Maple that I had been involved in a brawl with a group of drunks, and asked her to phone June that I should not be in. It was the lack of social incident in my life which slightly irritated Mrs Maple. She lived for gossip, and while she was sympathetic when she saw the results of the fight I could see that pleasurable excitement was mixed up in it. She offered to bring me up meals, and immediately put me on a bland diet as if I was suffering from a stomach complaint.

On the Monday my ankle still let me down. I read a large accumulation of Auction Catalogues, had a tasteless lunch of steamed fish and mashed potato, and fell asleep afterwards from sheer boredom. When I woke an hour or so later it was with the vaguest, tantalizing impression of a humiliating dream in which it had been impressed on me that I had committed the ultimate and unforgivable social gaffe. The details dissolved irrecoverably as I tried to sort them out, and I watched the darkening sky fitfully throw handfuls of snowflakes at my bedroom window.

When Mrs Maple came in she did not bear the invalid tea I had expected but a card. She handed it to me saying, 'The gentleman is downstairs,' with a significant nod which I knew was to convey that he was someone of importance. The card was engraved simply 'William T. Kelso', but this was underlined with a note in tiny crabbed writing, 'May I see you on an urgent business matter?'

Mr Kelso's steps were heavy and dragging. He began to speak as he came through my living-room, 'A few minutes of your precious time is all I crave,' and his voice was deep and grave. It was a surprise when a short, chubby figure came round the door. He was dressed completely in black, but his clothes were of the rather sharp kind that some American Catholic priests effect – his shoes and gloves were suède, and his hat had a wide band and a narrow brim. His glistening smooth hair was black and white like a badger's and grew low on his forehead, with an even stripe of white running back parallel with the meticulous parting. He had a mid-Atlantic accent but I thought he was Canadian.

He moved carefully across the room as if he was nursing a rupture. 'Good gracious! They said you were indisposed – I had no idea you had been severely wounded.'

'Oh, it's not serious,' I said, trying to sound modest.

He came up close and surveyed my face and neck. 'Kra-aazey,' he said in a lifeless sort of voice as if he did not know what he was saying. 'Te-errible,' he stressed, but sounded faintly disappointed.

He ignored the arm-chair I indicated and sat on a small bedside chair, which had never been used before, at first slumping down as if the close inspection of my cuts had been too much for him, then pulling himself up very straight, wrapping his overcoat carefully around his legs. He looked down at such an acute angle that I could not see his eyes, only the reflection of the light in his glasses.

'No, it's nothing really,' I insisted.

'That's just good old British phlegm, sir ...' He hesitated and his eyes wandered round the room.

'Your card said something about business,' I prompted.

'Yes, indeed. I negotiated your office stairs with circumspection. The old ticker, you know.' He felt his heart affectionately. 'And your assistant was kind enough to suggest I came here ... Well, to be brief, to the nub ... I wonder if you would be interested in buying a copy of Lenin's first book?' He jerked his head to have another quick look about him, the light flashing in his highly polished lenses.

'I would.' There had been an alacrity and eagerness in my tone which instantly I wished I could have taken back. Lenin's pamphlet *Workers of the World, Unite! Explanation of the law on Factory Fines* was first printed illegally in St Petersburg in 1895 on the secret press of *Narodnya Volya* (The People's Will), a terrorist organization. I had once made an unsuccessful bid on the second edition printed in Geneva in 1897 but I did not know that a copy of the first edition existed outside of the u.s.s.r. 'Is it the 1895 edition?' I asked.

He tapped his slightly greasy forehead as if the answer might tumble out. 'Yes, oh yes,' he said with a vague smile.

'Have you got it there?' I pointed to his black hide brief-case.

'No-o-o, I'm afraid it's too big – I could not get it in there.' He looked closely to see how this had gone down.

Doubt hovered in my mind. 'But that isn't so!' I exclaimed, feeling slightly irritated as well as disappointed. 'It is a small pamphlet, not more than fifty pages.'

'By Gad,' he said slowly, 'your words have the ring of authority. They do indeed.'

'I don't think you've seen the thing.'

'Ho-ho-ho,' he exclaimed seriously, the upper part of his waistcoat bouncing out rhythmically. 'A razor-sharp mind. Like a steel trap. I shall have to be careful treating with you, sir.'

'You're too kind,' I laughed.

'And you must forgive my harmless subterfuge. I wanted to see you and thought a rare book would be the abracadabraical approach. Don't be perturbed. We shall do business yet.' He removed his steel glasses to reveal cunning topaz eyes. 'Let me put this hypothetical case. Viz, you know the whereabouts of a certain rare book. Shall we say, for argument's sake, a first edition, delicately be-wrappered, of the immortal Lenin's work.' He laughed mirthlessly.

Disappointment on my part was being rapidly replaced by irritation.

'Mr Kelso, are you satisfied with the progress we are making on the "urgent business matter"?'

'Oh yes,' he replied decisively. He had dropped the Dr Johnson manner. 'We have got to know each other. Surely you would agree that is often an essential part of business. I feel I know a good deal about you, that I could only have learnt in these, well, modest surroundings, and by the invalid's bedside. Now, as I was saying, if you were on the trail of something in your own line of business and discovered you had a rival in the field, what would you do?'

'You have the advantage of me – you seem to know what you are talking about.'

He looked down at me with satisfaction, his black-gloved fingers sharply steepled. 'Bluntly then. We may be engaged in the same pursuit, competitors who might beneficially join forces ...' He opened his brief-case and took out some journals – *Chicago's Wood Products, Angewandtie Chemie, New York's Paper Trade Journal*, and plonked them down on the bed.

I frowned and made no comment. He fished about in the case again and extracted a piece of pink newspaper. It was a portion of a list of Stock Prices. From its alphabetical place in the column a name started out at me with cabalistic power: 'The Steyne Paper Co.'

Kelso sat back beaming, stretching his long top lip. 'Now, you're a literary man. You will allow me one allegory. Imagine a great octopus in its cave. Long tentacles weaving about untiringly, transmitting sensations to the brain which in turn says, "Get me that", "Crush that". One would be foolish indeed to approach the cave without formidable weapons. And what could be better than an ally who knows the secret weaknesses, the flaws in the armour?'

'Look, old man.' I said it in a particularly nasty way which I had rehearsed but never used since it had been demonstrated to me by a car salesman. 'I don't know what point you are trying to make, but I do know you haven't got a book to sell me. Do you mind going?'

'You mean that? You're certain?'

'Too right,' I said, raising myself up on my elbows. 'Lying in bed I am at rather a disadvantage, but I do mean it.'

He gave me a long thoughtful look before he replaced his glasses. 'I like you!' he said with studied surprise. 'You're perceptive, subtle.'

He repacked his magazines carefully. He closed his brief-case and thumped it with a gesture of satisfaction. 'You see, a mutual friend thought you might be embarking on a – foolish enterprise. One that yet another mutual – acquaintance tried. Well, now I think you won't ...'

On the way to the door he looked round to see that he had not left anything: his expression was benign and powerful. He spoke in a casual way. 'Where were you last Friday at 12.30? Ha! A purely rhetorical question and if you had replied my little trick would have been spoiled.' He pointed at me with a stubby forefinger. 'At 12.30 precisely you were standing on Piccadilly tube station, Bakerloo Line, the platform for Baker Street. Quite unaware I'm sure of a very large and powerful fellow standing just behind you. One adroit push then, you know, and your injuries would have been really serious. Most likely fatal.' He looked quite concerned for a second and then went out.

I murmured, 'Versteh, Willi.' I felt reasonably certain that this was the man to whom Berning had been talking on the phone when I went into his office at Splay, and even more sure that he would be one of Saul's closest advisers, probably outranking Berning. There were several disadvantages to implementing criminal acts at long distance. One would have to work through third parties who might be too slow and over-confident, like Des, or others who would not be infallible (despite the murderous blow, Stone had not died immediately: he might have lived long enough to expose the man behind the murderer). But the advantages were obvious, too. When Berning had drawn out from Kate my interest in Lupin and probed my connection with Stone, he would have reported back to Saul (the tentacle touching the possibly dangerous object with the answering message from the octopus's brain, 'Damage that – stop it'). And so I had been beaten up, and Kelso had been sent to underline this with an explanation, to make sure that nothing more drastic was necessary, and to add a final Warning. And what could I prove? That I had been involved in a fight at a party that I had received a visit from a doubtless reputable business man?

30

For a week after Kelso's visit I was in a continuously edgy mood; like someone with suspected cancer who has had a favourable verdict from a specialist yet cannot believe it. Even if William T. Kelso was convinced that I was harmless I doubted that his decision would be the final one. I put myself in Saul's position; he had been preyed on by two blackmailers, and now there was another one hovering about (or, at least, someone ferreting about in a way that threatened trouble). It was an odd situation that though I had not met Saul we both had reason to be frightened and suspicious of each other.

I toyed once again with the idea of going to the police, but my conviction that Saul had been responsible for the deaths of True and Stone was built up on a subtle relationship of gradually accumulated notions which I could not back up with facts. The only thing that I could show them to link Saul with True was the photograph which I had found at Victoria Villa, and that proved nothing by itself. I needed something concrete and convincing: if Stone had been cunning and cautious enough to leave a document which would incriminate his murderer, it had not come to light during Margaret's tidying up of his papers and my search through his secret shelves. I decided to make a careful study of his Journal to see if there were any overt or veiled references which I had overlooked in reading it fairly quickly.

As I made my way round London doing my routine work, attending auction sales, calling at bookshops, seeing customers, I discovered that in an apprehensive mood all kinds of things could take on a sinister, threatening aspect. If a street was deserted, I felt automatically that it would be a fine place for assassination by motor-cycle, and hurried along expecting to hear a powerful engine gunned and pointed at me. I kept close to the inside of the pavement on busy streets, and stood with my back to the wall when I waited on Underground stations. One thing had been expertly demonstrated to me – that murder by a seeming accident was a good method. I did not expect to be stabbed. But I did have a bad case of Charlie Hayteritis: while he thought that he was being kept under observation, I suspected that I might soon have a fatal accident.

It was deeply ironical that this should happen because of Saul, for I knew it would be a long time before I could forget his daughter. I wrote her three letters but destroyed them all.

This feeling of unease that the jovial, vulpine Kelso had left behind him reached a climax exactly one week after he had called at my flat. I was busy at my desk, collating a copy of Corbet's *Poetica Stromata*, and June was hurrying to finish some letters to catch the post. I heard unusually anguished breathing and heavy footsteps on the stairs, and wondered if it might be Kelso returned to deliver a revised opinion of my capacity for blackmail. But it was a handsome flat Indian face that appeared through the door. He remained in the tiny passage, apparently perplexed by the choice of doors, though there were only two, one of which was plainly marked 'w.c' and the other with my name-plate.

He lurched in out of breath, pointing to himself and mumbling, 'Narasingh Biswas.'

I nodded and waited for him to recover. He smiled at June, showing an excellent set of strong ivory-coloured teeth, and pushed back an unruly strand of long curly hair.

'Mr Robert Seldon, dealer in books ... exotica?'

'That's right. Were you looking for some specific book?'

He grinned widely as if I had made a naïve remark, and shot a quick look at June to see if she had picked up the joke but she was concentrating on her typing.

'My good friend Arunachalam, the well-known devotee of *Hatha Joga* ...' The sentence fizzled out as if he had lost interest in it and I noticed, with an unpleasant sensation, that his eyes were glancing quickly round the room, making an inventory, as Kelso had done in my flat. His eyes lighted without pleasure on my case of calf-bound seventeenth-century poets, the portrait of Thackeray and the Epstein bust of Shaw.

'My friend Arunachalam – suggested that your shop – a possible venue. You will understand that I shall never attain the *Jogi's Samadhi* – not sufficient control ...' This confusing statement ended in a suppressed giggle and rapid flickering of his right eyelid. He was giving off a heady smell of fried fish and lily-of-the-valley. When he saw that June was still bent over her notebook he nodded at her with another quick movement of his head to indicate that we should get rid of her.

I was anxious that she should remain. He appeared an inadequate assassin but he was in a state of barely controlled excitement that was rare in book collectors. Though it was a cold day, I could see little beads of sweat nestling among the oily ringlets at his temples.

'Mr Arunachalam has been here?' I said doubtfully.

'Oh no, no. But he gave me this.' Another meaningful look. He handed me a *Directory of Booksellers* open at the Mayfair section. A pencilled arrow and some greasy finger marks pointed to my entry, 'Robert Seldon – Rare & Interesting Books (XVIIth to XXth Century)'. The word 'interesting' had been underlined three times in green ink.

'You know,' he said, 'something amusin' – interesting – very jolly books ...' He spoke in spurts so that one had the impression of overhearing the chatter of a crowd.

He went up to one of the glass cases in irritation at my obtuseness, and looked along the rows, deleting the volumes one by one with an oblique movement of his finger as he read each title. He stuck a thick underlip over the upper one, to show that he was not pleased with the books.

'You know ...' he repeated, grimacing in an aggravated manner, interlacing his fingers and bobbing his head.

June got up, gathering letters. 'I shall just make it,' she said, disappearing downstairs.

'Oh, come on, Mr Seldon!' Mr Biswas leered in exasperation. 'We are both men of the world ... Amusin' books! The Frank Harris Life and Lovers. Fanny's Hill ...'

Most of my fear evaporated with Mr Biswas' disappointed retreat. I had been frightened of a collector of 'exotica' – I could descend no lower. It had the purgative effect of a peal of laughter on cowardly imaginings.

> Is all our Life, then, but a dream
> Seen faintly in the golden gleam
> Athwart Time's dark resistless stream?
>
> Bowed to the earth with bitter woe,
> Or laughing at some raree-show
> We flutter idly to and fro.
>
> Man's little Day in haste we spend
> And, from its merry noontide, send
> No glance to meet the silent end.

This poem by Lewis Carroll was the first entry in Stone's journal. It stood by itself in the middle of a page as an epigraph, and gave a suitably elegiac tone to the musings of a dead man. From its prominence and isolation it seemed safe to presume that these haunting lines had a special significance for Edward, but I was surprised that he had chosen a *Memento Mori* as a motto. He had always appeared so well contented with the various raree-shows that the world had to offer, whether he was handling a fine binding, chosing tobacco or wine, ordering a meal, or sniffing in the salt air at Sandbourne. 'Much to be thankful for', he had reminded me on occasion, and I should have said that he was a man well content with the world as it was, and not much bothered with thoughts of mortality. But then I had known him for a year without guessing that he was a homosexual. His subtlety and evasions had been too much for me.

There were 360 folio pages of fine white crisp paper, watermarked 'Original Turkey Mill', in the Journal, bound in dark blue cloth with a red leather spine, rather like an Accounts ledger. Some two hundred pages were filled with odd notes, thoughts, dry comments on human behaviour and quotations from Hardy, Montaigne, George Eliot, Donne and other authors I could not identify. Too many words in his large hand were crammed on to a page to make for

141

easy reading, and it was obvious that it had been written purely for the compiler's own satisfaction. At first sight it presented difficulties like a thick hedge: some sentences were contracted and others left unfinished, afterthoughts had been added in the margins and between lines.

It was on a bleak Saturday afternoon that I got down to a line-by-line reading of the manuscript. I had played a game of squash, had a brief swim in the pool at the courts, and returned to my flat to find it was only four o'clock. With a long evening to kill I decided to go through the Journal, exhaustively, making notes, looking up quotations and tracing allusions where I could. I did not find a word that Saul's lawyers would have thought compromising. It was true I came on a pregnant statement in March 1944: 'Interview with S. tomorrow' (three or four months after True's death Edward was in the position to confront the murderer); with my special knowledge I found this significant, but it could have referred to a dozen people with the initial S, and meant a hundred things.

The first dated entry, after the Carroll poem, was written on 4th January 1938 and related the details of his purchase of an 'Early Charter with a Monastic Seal. Reynald, Prior of Repton, *circa* A.D. 1230 ...' The last one had been written only a week before Edward was killed.

When I had been through the Journal previously I had tended to skim through the crowded pages, my eyes lighting mainly on references to the Ibiza letters. The methodical reading revealed an interesting attempt by Stone at a psychological analysis of 'R.B.T.'. It was preceded by a quotation from Thomas Hardy: 'A physician cannot cure a disease, but he can change its mode of expression.' I should want to add the proviso that the disease be of nervous origin – once that is done how well I know it to be true. The skin disease that is cured – and replaced by asthma. Migraines checked, but the sufferer develops an ulcer. All illness of that kind, it seems to me, is a form of protest by the individual against his environment. R.B.T., I think, was the perfect example of this. A captive of a brutalized imagination, serving out a life sentence in solitary confinement. Behind his mask there was a will that existed only for self-assertion and accepted therefore that any moment of 'success' would be one of disappointment. He was the gambler who wishes to lose – the schemer bent, unconsciously, on self-destruction. His illness was mental and its symptoms crime – the ludicrous early attempts at fraud were attended by a physician in the form of the Law, and when he was released from prison its 'mode of expression' had merely taken on a more subtle form.'

If I had been a perceptive detective, whole-heartedly bent on putting the jigsaw of the True–Stone–Saul crimes together, I should have cursed Stone for being so cautious even in his private journal that he did not say outright that True had become a blackmailer, or specify that his interview was with Saul. But my attitude was ambivalent – I could not make up my mind if I would do anything about the matter – and when I finally closed the book I did not know if I was really disappointed that there was no positive evidence.

31

SIX WEEKS after Stone's funeral, winter's grip was suddenly relaxed. It happened overnight: one evening the air was frosty, the next morning it was soft and warm, and there was some other difference, impossible to track down, in the atmosphere. Sounds of birds singing woke me at six and when I looked out I could see a few small fresh green shoots of snowdrops among the dun coloured grass under the hedge. I contrasted the bright inviting morning with the one on which I had gone to the sombre cemetery at Sandbourne; the landscape that day had appeared to be etched in black lines. The fat woman had said to me, 'It takes a funeral to make you appreciate being alive,' but it did not have that effect on me. It was the hardly perceptible first movements of spring that made me throw off a feeling of apathy. I decided to do a number of things that I had been putting off for weeks. I parcelled up Stone's Journal to be sent back by post, and wrote to Margaret explaining that I could not get down to Sandbourne for the time being. I had promised to do the probate valuation, but I intended to complete this from Pennington's figures.

When I had posted the parcel in the Strand I had a feeling of relief; while the Journal was of absorbing interest, I had always a sense of guilt in reading it, and this was dissipated finally when I had handed it over the counter. I knew that Margaret might well destroy it after glancing through a few pages: notes about books, and quotations from others, were of no interest to her. But I was glad to leave the decision to her. I spent the morning at Hodgson's and got back to my office just before 12.30 when June was due to go for lunch. As I went up the last flight of stairs I could hear her laughing, and I expected to find one of her guardee friends waiting to take her to an Italian restaurant she favoured, making desultory smart conversation and poking an umbrella into my carpet.

Instead of the imagined bowler-hatted tall thin shape, there was the small chunky one of Rudolph Bergl sitting in the arm-chair, his short legs not quite touching the floor, gazing with undisguised admiration at June. There was an atmosphere of pleasant intimacy which rather surprised me, but I knew I continually under-estimated June's ability for getting on with rather unconventional people. I tried to imagine what work Bergl did: being conductor of the Finchley Grove Orchestra did not sound like a full-time occupation.

As I went in June got up and pointed at me. 'Do excuse me, Mr Bergl. Mr Seldon, you had a phone call – two, in fact, from the same woman. I asked if you could ring her back but she said it wasn't possible. She said she would try again about one o'clock.'

I guessed it might be Margaret who had phoned. If we met again in suitable surroundings, I knew that it could end in the same result as the last time: I could conjure up mental pictures of her which I found exciting; at the same time, 'love-making' without love was an empty business.

Bergl put an end to my thoughts about Margaret by holding out to me a book-shaped parcel and a letter. 'Mrs St Clair asked me to give you these.' The letter was in a large blue envelope, addressed in a bold florid hand.

'It is a gift,' Bergl said. 'Are you surprised?'

'Well,' I admitted, 'I didn't think we got on all that well. In fact, I thought she found me ...'

'Ah, you're wrong,' he interrupted in a tone of dry, flat amiability. 'You don't understand her. Naturally. It takes time. She was rather on edge when you called. You know how people are when they are selling things. Rather anxious. They don't know how much they are worth and so on.'

'Yes, but I hardly expected a present.'

'There is an explanation.' He waved a packet of cigarettes at June and then at me: when we refused he lit one, half closing his eyes against the smoke, retreating behind it for an instant. He had big brown sceptical eyes and a vaguely continental manner.

'It's – h-m, how shall I put it? Mrs St Clair – May – has clairvoyant powers. We have regular séances. Her control, Black Feather, suggested that' – he gave a thin embarrassed laugh – 'this was a propitious time for a friendly act.'

I stifled a snort.

'You don't believe in anything like that?' he asked.

'Frankly, no. I think it's a lot of malarkey.'

'You can't be sure,' June volunteered, and gave me a candid look.

'Sometimes – I suspend belief myself,' Bergl said in a conciliatory tone. 'But I've got to be going. Oh, by the way, May said that you should read the letter first. Apparently it explains the contents of the parcel.'

He went out with June and I heard them chattering down the stairs. I reached for Mrs St Clair's letter just as the phone began to ring. 'Is Mr Seldon there now?' It was a diffident, quiet voice that I did not recognize.

'Yes – Seldon speaking.'

'Oh – it's Kate Saul. I'm in London and I thought I might call at your office, but it's too late now.'

'Too late?' I automatically and foolishly glanced at my watch to see that it was ten past one.

'Well, yes. You see, I'm flying to Switzerland this afternoon and I'm just going off to the Air Terminal.' There was a moment of silence. When she spoke again her voice was toneless and pitched even lower: 'My father died yesterday.'

As she said that, many thoughts and sensations contended in my brain. Fellow feeling above all, for I did know how she felt: the bewilderment, and the sensation of being lost. Sympathy – for her unusual sensitivity was tied up with complete vulnerability. Vividly I remembered walking back to the station after I had seen our bombed house; each street, each shop had touched off intolerably sad memories of my family. So now would Kate be affected. But in among these feelings there was also one of relief. Kelso's 'octopus' was destroyed – there was no more need for fear; and I could finally forget the distasteful idea of revenge. All this in a few seconds while silence hung between us again.

'How terrible!' I could be sincere in saying this as my feeling was for her and not the dead man. 'It must have been very sudden. I thought you said he was rather better when I saw you at Splay ...'

'Yes – no warning at all.' There was a flaw in her voice and I sensed that she was balanced on the edge of tears. 'He just had another stroke. And my sister is in Canada – that makes it worse. I was trying to contact her all yesterday afternoon and evening, but it was no good.'

'Look, could I come and see you at the terminal? I could get there in ten minutes, and I might be able to come out to the airport. Where are you going?'

'Zürich. Yes, do come if it's not too much trouble. I'm feeling rather overwhelmed. The prospect of dealing with everything ...'

'Don't let it get you down. Where are you now?'

'A hotel in Kensington.'

'Right. I'll get a taxi and I'll probably be at the terminal before you are ...'

After I had replaced the phone my head buzzed with ideas. There had been something in her tone that made me feel I could help her, and the sensation of being wanted was a rare one in my life. I took my passport and some money from the desk and scribbled a note to June, then dashed down the stairs at such a speed that my weak ankle rebelled by the time I had reached the ground floor. I caught a taxi in Conduit Street still clutching my passport and Mrs St Clair's letter and box. The letter sprawled over three pages.

Dear Mr Seldon,

Mr Hayter has told me that you are particularly interested in Lupin's letters to 'Paolo'. I think I can sate your curiosity on that score. 'Paolo' was the rather ridiculous nickname given by Lupin to my husband Charles. You may be surprised that I tell you this, but you are such a persistent person that I am sure you would eventually ferret it out. And indeed, there must be some school friends of Charles still alive who would remember that Lupin called him that at school. As you are so well up in the Lupin 'canon' you may not need to be told that Lupin

147

was dismissed from his post as master at a well-known public school in 1908. My husband first came under his evil domination when he was thirteen years old. Perhaps you will understand now how I feel about Lupin and his influence.

My husband died in 1940. The 'Ibiza' letters were not among his possessions then. They were sent to me, anonymously, only a few years ago by some ironist who no doubt found it amusing to forward such sophisticated filth to the widow of the recipient. My gravamen against that unholy crew is their horrible habit of flaunting their beastliness.

'Pervert' is a good name for someone who tries to make a virtue of an inadequacy. However, I have dealt fairly with these relics of their High Priest. Lupin, dear Charles, and the detestable Lamplugh are all dead. So are most of the other 'men' who were mentioned therein. May the matter now rest?

Sincerely yours,
May St Clair

I ripped off the brown paper and found a large cigar box. It had been chosen with care to fit a blue morocco binding with FREDERICK S. LUPIN in gilt Trajan letters on the front cover. I lifted the binding out and found it was empty. The pages had been cut out with a razor, leaving only stubs of the leaves of stiff paper and guards inserted to protect them. At the bottom of the box there was an inch of dull grey ash.

May St Clair had dealt firmly with the letters, as she had done with other relics of the past. Her husband had been a homosexual in his youth and had left her in middle age. Now she was busy suppressing evidence of both inadequacies. She had made a museum of relics that showed him as a normal boy, young man and husband. The others went into the fire. I heard myself say, 'The old witch!' But there was admiration mixed up with my annoyance.

I replaced the binding case gently on its bed of ashes so that they would not spurt out over the floor of the taxi, then put the box and the paper wrapping on the seat, to puzzle the next occupant.

The set-up would appeal to Bernard Orville's sardonic sense of humour: I had the Ibiza letters in my hands but could not ask a penny for them. Any other afternoon I should have kept the binding to show how tantalizingly close I had come to making an easy £500; but on my way to see Kate again, the bizarre situation of Lupin and his letters seemed quite unimportant.

If Kate was willing, I was going to suggest that I should fly to Zürich with her. I had the excuse that I had often visited the city on business and knew it well; my German was fluent, and I hoped to be able to help her. Never before had I decided on an impulse to go somewhere without plans or pyjamas. If Kate would give me a word of encouragement I was going to try something else that was new for me – looking forward, not back.